Pairs

WITH

Pinot

Mary Ann Tippett

ISBN: 978-1-7753883-2-6 (Paperback)

First printing edition 2019.

PREFACE

The dating application questions in the following fictional story were derived from an actual study* conducted by Dr. Arthur Aron; noted social psychologist, whose work focuses on friendship and intimacy in relationships.

To test his self-expansion model, Dr. Aron paired unacquainted individuals and gave them specific questions to ask each other.

One of the pairs fell in love and eventually married.

---

*Aron A., Melinati E., Aron E.N., Vallone R.J. & Bator R. (1997). *The Experimental Generation of Interpersonal Closeness: A Procedure and Some Preliminary Findings.* [Viewed April 2018] Personality and Social Psychology Bulletin, 23, 363-377.

"A soulmate is the one person whose love is powerful enough to motivate you to meet your soul, to do the emotional work of self-discovery, of awakening."

– Kenny Loggins

1
FAITH

1. Given anyone in the world, whom would you want as a dinner guest?

|

Faith presses a loose lock of frizzy blonde hair behind her ear and imagines speaking definitively to her date. Not just a date. Her soulmate date. Just write what pops into your head, she tells herself. Don't overthink it.

Jesus.|

No wait, scratch that. She can't sit through dinner without wine. Jesus is not a wine drinker. Except he did turn water into wine. So maybe he drinks it too. But no. Who wants to date a girl who wants to have dinner with Jesus?

Except she should be honest, she chides herself. Her soul-mate will be attracted to her authentic self. Her answers should be genuine. Off the cuff. Reflective of who she is.

Except wait. The algorithm, or whatever it's called that sorts her answers into soulmate attracting digests, well it probably accounts for dishonesty. Propensity for dishonesty on these things is built in, isn't it?

Jesus, this is hard.

Faith rereads the question. Given anyone *in the world*. Okay, phew. Jesus is other-worldly. Right? For sure.

Robert Parker would be interesting, she thinks. But no, there would be too much talk about wine. Too much sniffing and swirling and bouquet-ing. And he's old. Besides, mixing work with love would be weird. Not that dinner guest means potential love interest. This is just a question about who I find interesting, she thinks. Come on, focus here.

"Don't you work today?"

Bitta is standing in the doorway of Faith's room. Bitta's room, actually. Faith has called her grandmother Bitta, short for Grandma Elizabeth, since she can remember.

Faith pats her dampish hair. Soon the frizz will be permanent and uncooperative with the blow dryer. "Yes. Just working on the app questionnaire," Faith says.

Bitta's furrowed brow unfurrows. "So you decided to take the extra week?" she asks, plopping the morning newspaper onto the bed next to Faith. The "Jobs" section glares from the top of the stack.

Faith glances at her Wine Studies diploma that Bitta framed and set on her tiny bedside table. It is dwarfed by a quirky polka-dotted lamp towering over its fragile stand, but the grad date looms large. Bitta gave her a year to save some money while she looked for a "real" job. Two weeks left. Three if she gives this new dating app a try. "Who knows?" her grandma had said. "You might find a sugar daddy, get knocked up, and forget about a job for a while."

Faith rolls her eyes. "You know, I'm still grieving here. Shouldn't you be more sympathetic?"

"It's been five years. Life goes on," Bitta says. "Tick-tock," she adds, before lumbering off toward the kitchen, purposely leaving the door wide open.

Faith shakes her head and tries to tuck a piece of frizz behind her ear again. She may have missed the blow-drying window, she thinks. Okay, focus. Just get this one question over with. She hears Jasper stirring up fluff. The room is so small that her gerbil's amusement park-like cage takes up the entire corner

3

space between the foot of her bed and the wall. Faith sets down her laptop and crawls to the end of the bed to check on him. "Morning, Jasper."

He's half out of his loft nest, running tiny claws over his head like a man in a shower, pausing a fraction of a second to dip one hand then another in his mouth. My soulmate will have to like animals, Faith thinks. She conjures up a picture of a rugged Australian type, bearded and jovial, who scoops her into a warm embrace after the two of them set a trapped mink free. Are there minks in Australia? Maybe a trapped wallaby – do people trap those?

She grabs her laptop and plops on to her stomach to type, the newspaper falling open to the current events section as she does so. A journalist would be interesting, Faith thinks. Someone who asks questions for a living, visits unusual places, forms unbiased opinions based on listening. Surely my soulmate is a good listener. Quickly, she googles famous handsome journalists. Mmmm, yummy, she thinks, when she finds the one.

Given anyone in the world, whom would I want as my dinner guest? She types:

> David Muir.|

She drinks in the image on her computer screen a few more seconds, then adds:

> David Muir. With a beard.|

✱✱✱

Thanks to missing the blow-dry window, Faith banks twenty minutes, allowing her to arrive early for her shift as cashier at Farm Boy. She stands in front of four boxes of wine that arrived in the night. The first is from Henry of Pelham. Henry of "Phlegm," one of her profs used to call it. She likes their simple fruit-forward wines, though, recognizing her palate is young and yet to evolve.

"Hey, Curly." Chad erupts through the swinging doors behind her, stamping his wet high-tops on the industrial strength shred of carpet beneath the time clock.

Faith fluffs at her hair like a primping beauty contestant. "You like? It's all the rage in wintery trends." She points at the wine boxes. "You okay if I steal your job again?"

Chad finds his card and stamps it in the machine. *Ker-chunk*. "Fill your boots. I'll grab a smoke outside then." He pulls up his hoodie and removes a joint from his pocket.

Faith shakes her head as she picks up the box and places it on the trolley. Chad pockets the joint and helps her load the other three. "I don't get how secretly stocking wine will help you get one of those fancy wine careers," he says. "Cashier is easier. And pays better."

"Ha ha," Faith intones. "This is the first grocery allowed to sell wine in Ontario. And I have a wine degree. So…"

"That and five bucks will buy you a cup of coffee," Chad says, chuckling as he disappears through the doors to the loading dock.

Faith has a deal with Chad. She gets to do his wine related tasks. And in return, she doesn't rat him out for smoking-up on the clock. In truth, he knows she wouldn't rat him out anyway. But he is young and lazy and knows a good gig when he sees it.

Carefully, she wheels the trolley through the double doors, navigates the awkward turns around the store perimeter past the bakery where she waves at Stella, who labours over some focaccia dough, before she finally arrives at the front corner near the snacks. The humble assortment of wine shelving has grown from half of one snack-wall to both walls of the corner since she started working here a year ago.

Grocery cashier was supposed to be a temporary job while she hunted down a top salary position in export management. Those positions, it turns out, are few and far between and require expensive plane tickets to Toronto or Vancouver to interview for, not that she's ever landed an interview. They also require experience. And university degrees. And often post-university degrees. Her college degree barely gets her in the door for hotel hospitality jobs, and none of those so far feature wine as a skill set.

When she finally adjusted her employment inquiries, targeting Cellar Hand, LCBO Clerk, and Wine Production Assistant type positions, she got more nibbles. Weeks later, she accepted the cashier position at a wine-selling grocery: close enough to her dream career.

Bitta seemed to instantaneously smell her defeated attitude like a hound on a wounded rabbit. "You are too young to settle," she said. Then she reminded her to look for apartments and potential roommates, because "tick-tock."

Faith removes half of the slow-selling wine brands, and fills the spaces with the newer labels selected by the store's Wine Buyer. When she's done, she stands back and admires the scene. Crisp whites on the far left, golden Chardonnays on the right, pale to ruby coloured Rosés in the middle. Around the corner on the right wall, a sea of delightful reds, the more vibrant labels at eye level.

Ka-ching. She hears one of the cashiers setting up a register. Faith closes the half-empty wine boxes with swift precision and steers the trolley, much lighter now, directly through the widest vegetable aisle to the back of the store. Chad is ready with his labeler. She hands off the trolley and gives him winery and varietal information for the new shelf sections, then picks up her cash bag from the office and makes it to her station with three minutes to spare.

As the first few customers dribble into the store, Faith gazes at the snowflakes softening her strip mall vista and watches them melt into puddles between the cars. The Tim Hortons across the street disappears behind a dotted blanket of grey and white before her eyes. And in its place she imagines a handsome stranger on a snowbank, fending off a band of poachers from attacking the wide-eyed baby seals behind him.

2
BRIAN

Brian Lovelace nearly collides with a business suit type on his way into The Barley Mow. "Sorry," he mumbles.

Brushing at his lapel, the Suit fixes his perturbed face into a polite grimace-smirk. "Slow down there, eh?"

"Sorry," Brian says again. "I'm late." The two of them momentarily trapped by civilities in the foyer.

The Suit nods congenially and makes to escape, one hand on the outer door, a steady gust of wind fighting his effort to leave. Brian is part-way through the inner door, between pub-furnace heat and soul-numbing cold, when Suit touches his elbow. "The road to oblivion is paved with excuses," he says with a wink.

"Brian!" Jenson yells. He's sitting with Vivia, a vacant bar stool between them, at the bar's furthest arc. "Over here!" he shouts again, pointing enthusiastically to the empty bar stool.

Brian waves. He holds the door open a beat longer, surveying the chaotic assembly of students, semi-codgers like himself and couples.

What does that even mean, *road to oblivion*, Brian wants to know. Isn't it *Hell and good intentions* or something like that? But when he turns the Suit is gone, a puddle of slush settling over his Blundstone imprint on the floor mat. Brian runs his fingers through the snow-encrusted beard near his chin, brushing off the odd encounter while picking his way carefully through the raucous Thursday night crowd.

He claps Jensen on the back and greets Vivia with their customary two-cheek kiss. "Tell me why we're at this place?" Brian asks, as he wedges onto the stool through a cluster of spirited university students.

"Wing night," Jensen says, feigning offence. He waves his arm over the greasy baskets in front of Vivia and himself. Vivia holds up a bony morsel, her darkly framed eyeglasses a smeary rainbow, and Jensen taps his last wing against hers in *Cheers* fashion.

"And if a person doesn't like fried bits of bird joints?"

Just then a board studded with four small wine glasses appears before Brian. "Pinot, pinot, cab, cab," the harried bartender points out and moves on to the pretty blonde crushing in behind Brian for her order.

"Wine flights – also on special," Vivia announces over Jensen who has suddenly draped himself across the bar, fishing for something on the other side.

"Pub wine. Excellent," Brian muses, his anxiety loosening. At least he won't have to find a blueberry beer and pretend to like it.

"Today's selection," Jensen adds, plunking a placard in front of him, highlighting the small-pour overpriced varietals Brian knows he would walk right by at the LCBO.

The blonde behind Brian reaches for her pink-hued wine, simultaneously handing over her credit card and accepting the overfull glass with one hand from the bartender. Brian feels her billowy chest nestle into his back. She smiles when she sees Brian's flight. "Ooo," she says, "a connoisseur! What do you recommend?"

Brian leans away to avoid the wine sloshing out of her glass as she speaks. She is young, an undergrad looking for free drinks. "I'm partial to Pinot Noir," he says.

The bartender returns with a receipt for the girl. "Cheers!" she says, holding her glass too close to Brian's stainable leather jacket. He picks up one of the tiny Cabernets and delicately clinks the glass against hers.

"I think she likes you," Jensen says, after she retreats into the crowd. "Why didn't you ask her name?"

"Come on, Jensen," Brian sips from the Cab, recoiling at its cloying fruitiness before setting it down again. "I have a girlfriend." *Oblivion.* The word pecks at his mind.

"When are you going to dump her?" Vivia says. She's been trying to catch the bartender's eye. She tentatively waves her empty beer glass, as he does a flyby. "She said no. Even I know that's code for move on."

"She's just not ready for marriage yet. Besides, it's not worth the heartache putting myself out there." *Oblivion. Like Oblivious.* How are excuses connected to obliviousness? "You know what I'm talking about, 'eh Vivia?"

Her eyes widen just enough to register the sting. Jensen slaps his hands on the bar. "Enough of the unlucky at love talk! It's wing and flight night. Drink up, Brian."

"Fine," Brian says, letting the angst about his love-life dissipate with a sip of Pinot. He didn't expect much complexity in a Pub Pinot, but he is immediately disappointed when this one fails to surprise.

"Listen," Jensen says, "Vivia and I were talking about that new dating app, SoulMate."

"The one *guaranteed*," Brian says with air quotes, "to connect you with your one true love?"

"Right," Jensen says, his crystal blue eyes twinkling with delight. "You know the one, good." He takes a swig of beer and continues, speaking quickly. "Well, obviously it's a crock. We're thinking we should do an exposé piece on it."

"You have a contact on the inside?"

"No, no, that's no fun. One of us needs to sign up, and when we don't find the love of our life, get our money back. You know, figure out what the angle is as we go, so to speak."

"Not me though," Vivia adds. "I can't deal with rejection right now."

"Steele will never go for it," Brian says, "and I have my hands full with the cannabis legislation."

"The bill passed," Jensen says. "You have time." He digs into a fresh basket of wings. "And Steele's already signed off on it," He waves a wing around like a conductor.

"One, the bill is not law yet. There are plenty of stories around police ignoring flagrant pot-selling shops. Two, I'm a political reporter. You are Ottawa's award-winning fluff writer." Jensen smiles and takes a barstool bow.

"And most importantly..." Brian picks up the other Pinot, sniffs at it, frowns and sets it down again. "...I have a girlfriend." He sees Jensen and Vivia exchange eye-rolls. "Just because you don't like Tanica doesn't mean she's wrong for me."

Jensen and Vivia contemplate their beer glasses.

"What do you guys know, anyway?" Brian continues. "You sleep with anyone that moves," he says to Jensen. "Have you even had a relationship?"

Jensen opens his mouth to object.

"And you," Brian says to Vivia. "Have you ever made it past two dates?"

Vivia looks down at her wing basket miserably. Jensen pats her hand. "Sling mud if you like," he says, "but you are the only one who actually wants a lasting relationship right now. What do you have to lose?"

"Tanica. That's what." Brian drinks the too fruity Cab like a shot. *Oblivion*, he thinks, as he sets the glass down too hard. "Listen, can we do a real restaurant next week? One with a proper wine list at least?"

"Sure, you pick," Jensen says. "But download the app. Please? Promise to think about it?"

Brian looks away, scans the crowd of couples and young people strutting their assets. The lascivious energy is almost tangible. Lately couples seem to swarm around him with their excessive eye gazing and relentless hand-holding and PDA limb-entangling. He and Tanica had that once. But they have moved beyond that now, graduated to the safer zone of contentment, safe from the passion-laced torrents that infect budding relationships.

"What's she up to tonight, anyway?" Vivia asks, changing the subject. She is wiping her fingers on a wet-nap while Jensen signals for the bill.

"She has a thing," Brian says, trying to recall exactly what she said. Girls night? Girl meeting? Meeting? *Oblivious.* He is beginning to hate that word. It needs to stop being in his head. What's the opposite of oblivion? Awareness? From now on, he will think only of awareness.

"Oh that's nice," Vivia says. "You meeting up later?" She places the wet nap in the basket and brushes a phantom crumb off her lap.

"I told her we'd be out late," Brian lies. "I'll see her tomorrow."

Vivia and Jensen exchange a look. Brian fights off the word before it lands – I am *aware* they disapprove, he thinks. Fully aware. Could not be more aware. Take that, *oblivious.* Fuck.

"Well," Jensen says, collecting his receipt. "You owe me $23.50, and the night is young. Where to?"

Brian looks at his watch. 10 p.m. is not late. "Pinball and perogies?"

"Please no," Viv says. "Last time I hooked up with a girl there, and I'm still waiting for a text. Or Instagram follow. Or any sign of life."

"Seinfeld trivia at Black Squirrel then?" Brian offers.

Jensen sticks his hands in the air guiltily. "I did some cavorting with a waitress there. Two, actually. Made the air in the place a bit chilly."

The three sit in silence a few seconds, arriving at the solution simultaneously without words.

"Fine," Brian says. "But I haven't eaten. Can we grab popcorn from the Mayfair first?"

"Oh yeah! Extra-large, extra butter," Vivia says.

***

They dust off the snow from their usual bench by the frozen Rideau River and share a joint. Wind threatens to steal their popcorn as the bag gets lighter and lighter. Their gloves are caked with gelled butter, but Brian's fingers are warm underneath.

"Is it normal to like sex so much?" Jensen asks. His speech is slow and melancholy.

"It's in our DNA to like sex," Vivia offers. "Is that a cop?" They turn to assess the same homeless person she asked about moments before. He is draped across a picnic table behind them, covered in sleeping bags.

"For the third time, no," Brian says.

"Maybe fourth," puts in Jensen.

Vivia looks over her shoulder again. "Maybe we should move."

"He's oblivious," Brian says. "Obliterated. Obviously."

"You keep saying that word," Jensen says.

"What word?"

"Oblivion. And other words with *obv*."

Brian considers this. He allows his mind to ponder the word freely now. "How is oblivion related to excuses?"

"He just moved," Vivia says, looking over her shoulder.

They all look. "Nope. Wind ruffling his covers." Jensen says. "Vivia is not oblivious," he directs this at Brian. "She makes no excuses for not being oblivious."

"I hate double negatives," Vivia says. "There are no double negatives in financial reporting."

They ponder this and start giggling. "That makes no sense," Brian says. "Let's make it positive for fun. Hmm. She makes excuses for being oblivious." He says it slowly, stressing each syllable. "There."

"I see it now," Jensen says.

"I told you. He moved," Vivia says, pivoting around to stare the picnic table clump down.

Jensen ignores her. "Excuses relate to oblivion. How. That's what I see."

"You said 'how.' But you didn't say how," Brian says. He scratches his toque. While he's at it, he pulls it down more over his ears. That's better.

"How. Hmmm," Jensen says, while tapping Vivia on her shoulder.

She turns around. "What?"

"If you are oblivious," he asks, "do you make excuses?"

"We should move," she says.

"Oh I see it too," Brian says. "If I'm oblivious and I know it, I'll make excuses about the things I'm oblivious to."

They sit in silence. A semi-trailer rumbles loudly down the road across the river. The homeless man's snores become back-up music to the traffic sounds.

"That doesn't make sense," Jensen finally says.

"That's it. I'm moving," Vivia says.

✳✳✳

1. Given anyone in the world, whom would you want as a dinner guest?

> |

Well, that's easy, Brian thinks, and writes:

> Donald Trump.
>
> (Can he really be that bad? I mean, come on.)|

He still can't believe he got talked into this. He woke up early this morning, curled up next to Tanica. No memory of her coming home. He made a fresh pot of coffee and checked emails, noticing the bright, shiny new app Jensen downloaded for him when his attention was diverted elsewhere. In the clear morning light, he realized there is no harm in creating a profile.

He has to admit the cannabis reporting has grown stale. No one is shocked about it anymore. It's a given. With each article he writes, he can picture the reader's eyes glazing over, moving on to the next item. To something more relevant, something up-in-arms worthy.

As the sun climbed higher, he sipped his coffee, answered emails, and enjoyed the icy river views from his favourite window chair, an aromatic cup of Happy Goat java steaming from his mirror-topped coffee table. Emailing complete, he spent some time researching the app, and its creators. He found surprisingly little, other than the canned press releases concerning the app's success: The scientific statistical advantage it has over its competitors; the patented technology protecting its secret formula garnering more hits than misses. Curious, he abandoned the research and clicked on the app.

So far, the app fails to impress. The first round of questions is typical profile stuff – name, date of birth, gender identity, gender preference, sphere of residence, education and background, etc. The second round of questions takes him back to post-graduate first-apartment parties when university-era friends would gather on weekends. Inevitably, the latest trend in board games would be unearthed, questions meant to expose embarrassing thoughts and opinions would be aired, martini glasses refilled, and before the last die rolled, someone would become silently sullen at best or fuming mad and teary at worst, bringing an awkward end to the night.

These are the types of questions rarely asked in isolation. They are meant to be asked in a contemplative moment among friends. Or on a therapist's couch. Before he can push on to the next question, he sees Tanica making her way from the floor above, her graceful steps encircled by a wisp of creamy satin she gathers around her as she descends.

"Good morning, sleepy-head," Brian says, "Late night?"

Tanica's smile fails to reach her eyes. "I could ask you the same," she says, a morning rasp in her voice. "Coffee?"

Brian points to a tiny cup atop the espresso machine. The faded froth on her macchiato was perfect when he made it. But they are long past arguing over timing and frothing and competing coffee-making strategies. "How was your thing?" he asks.

She floats past the so-old-it's-new-again dining table to the kitchen and picks up the cup with its saucer, smelling the no-doubt tepid liquid dramatically. "That's the good stuff," she says. Like she always says. "It was fine. How was your thing?"

Brian watches her take her first sip, a stab of unease niggling at him. He knows what she likes, right? He's a good provider. *Oblivion* pops into his head again. "It was okay. Met Jensen and Viv at a pub. Drank some forgettable wine." He decides to skip the part about smoking on the bench. He knows she is skeptical about marijuana and its harmlessness. "I bumped into a man on my way in. He said the strangest thing. It's still bouncing around in my head though. Has that ever happened to you? A comment from a stranger that takes on a life of its own in your mind?"

Tanica has the fridge open. She takes out an apple and gives him a quizzical glance. "How do you mean?" She sets the apple on the marble white bar that forms an austere island in the kitchen. She pulls a cutting board from below the sink and starts to slice the apple.

"I said 'excuse me' or 'sorry' or something like that and he replied that 'the road to oblivion is paved with excuses.'"

"Sounds like the ramblings of a drunk man," Tanica says, as she slices.

Brian considers the logic and convinces himself she is right. He has been fixating on the ramblings of a drunk person. "It's just that he didn't seem drunk," he says out loud without meaning to.

Tanica carries on with her slicing without comment. He watches her carefully place the slices in a parfait glass then dab a spoonful of yogurt on top, followed by a sprinkle of granola. He didn't notice her take the yogurt from the fridge. Or the granola from the baking drawer.

"Vivia asked about you," he says. "She wanted to know what you were up to." Tanica places the cutting board and knife in the dishwasher then pushes her breakfast across the bar before walking around to a stool on the other side. "I'm embarrassed to say I couldn't remember what you were doing last night," Brian adds, pretending to focus more on his laptop than the answer he is waiting for.

Brian scrolls to the next question on the SoulMate app and attempts to read it, his mind spinning elsewhere. Tanica quietly spears an apple and takes her time chewing it. He tries not to notice when she swallows, sips her coffee, and starts to spear another without comment.

"What was it again?" Brian says.

She stops mid-spear and looks at him like he's just entered the room. "What was what?"

"The thing you had last night. What was it again? I said I was embarrassed I didn't remember when Vivia asked."

Tanica lets the fork drop with a clang and slides off the stool. "You still don't fucking trust me, do you?" she says, and drifts back up the stairs.

3
FAITH

2. In what way would you like to be famous, if at all?

|

amous for being famous, Faith thinks. Not like the movie stars and pop artists whose lives are not their own. More like one of those reality TV people or Paris Hilton. Whatever happened to her, she wonders? Maybe she's not famous anymore. Faith realizes she hasn't read a People magazine in months, maybe years. She will totally subscribe when she has disposable income, she decides. A person should know whether Paris Hilton is still pulling attention-seeking hijinks or is old, boring and forgotten. She supposes that's what Google is for. But still, how much googling can a person do before they lose all focus on anything important? So, reality star famous it is, but only if she is one of those generally considered super nice and super smart types. And only if she becomes famous apologetically, rejecting all perks that come with being famous as a philosophical protest of sorts.

"Break's over," Stella says, bumping through the loading dock door. She shakes the snowflakes off her coat and walks over to the time clock to punch in.

Faith gets up from her chair by the supply boxes. She already misses the bench out front where she took her breaks in the summer. There are no benches on the loading dock, and the smoke is usually too intense even if there were. She keeps the app open on her phone so she can at least finish Question 2. "Let me ask you something, Stella." She grabs her card and punches it. "Would you rather be reality TV famous or movie star famous?"

Stella laughs, a congenial guffaw that stirs up the skin under her chin. "Neither," she says. "I've seen how they act. Not a moment's peace. Can't even maintain a marriage, most of 'em." She removes a small bottle of sanitizer from her pocket and rubs it into her fingers, then offers it to Faith.

"No, thank you," Faith says. She smiles warmly at Stella. "You really love your Ralph, don't you?"

Another guffaw from Stella, as she sprays a beach-scented mist over her baker's hat and blouse. "Course I love 'im." She offers the spray to Faith, who declines. "I mean, been together since high school. We ain't like those cheesy, lusty, freshly in love couples that moon about all over the grocery aisles. I mean, it's kind of cute." She stares off wistfully for a moment. "And kinda makes me want to vomit," she adds, levelling her seasoned grimace at Faith.

Faith can't help but laugh at that. She has seen more and more couples like Stella mentions, come to think of it. And she wonders if that's a sign she is spending too much time dwelling on this silly SoulMate app and its questions. "You are nothing if not honest," Faith says. "Thanks for your input." She taps her phone to refresh and writes:

> Famous for being famous.
>
> The reality TV kind. Apologetically famous. Respected.|

"Whatcha doin' there?" Stella asks, peering over her shoulder. "That ain't that SoulMate app, is it?"

Faith blushes. "You caught me. It's kind of embarrassing."

Stella just stands there, her incredulous body language demanding more of an explanation.

"I'm doing it under duress," Faith continues.

She stops to let Chad squeak around them with an oil-thirsty trolley on his way to the supply boxes. Faith lowers her voice. "Bitta's kicking me out in two weeks. But she's bribing me with an extra week if I go through with this SoulMate thing. She's worried my biological clock is ticking."

She looks over at Chad, who is loading boxes a little too quietly. Then puts her arm around Stella to draw her closer. "I wouldn't mind finding a soulmate," she whispers, "but I don't see how an app will solve my problems."

"Hmmph," Stella says. She unravels from the half hug and takes Faith's chin into her meaty hands. "Don't expect a man to solve your problems," she says as sternly as possible. Faith rubs some flour from her cheek as Stella ambles toward the doors. Before leaving she adds, "There's something in the air though since that app came about, I'll tell you that."

As the doors sway to a close, Chad pipes in, "You don't need an app to get a date." He loads the last of the boxes, as he speaks. Then he looks at her with alarm in his eyes, like he can't believe she forced him to talk, like he wants to take the comment back with all his heart. "I mean...sorry," he says, squeak-rolling past her to the doors. "Mind your own business. That's what my mom says," he mumbles with an awkward laugh, his face beet red as he leaves.

"Are you around tonight?" Faith texts Allie.

Allie lives next door to Bitta. They've been best friends since high school, after Faith's mom died. Faith had no choice other than moving in with her grandmother. Her father made a drunken appearance at the funeral, saw there was no money to bequeath to estranged husbands, let alone a daughter, and promptly disappeared again. Faith had to change schools in Grade 10 when she moved to Bitta's, which was awkward and lonely. But Allie, whose family knew Bitta from church, showed up the first day of school with an extra Herschel backpack for Faith when she heard Bitta had deemed a giant camping backpack from the basement garage sale pile as good enough. They have been best friends ever since.

They even went to the same college, Allie finding a job right away as a paralegal, Faith not so much. When they discovered that the house next to Bitta is a secret haven for abused women, Allie orchestrated a dramatic falling out with her boyfriend (who she didn't like much anyway), and as luck would have it, slipped on some ice shortly afterwards. Drawing on her theatrical talents (she was lead in the high school play), Allie earned the last spot in the shelter next door with her dramatic abuse story and broken arm.

"Yep," Allie texts back. "Back door at 6?"

They always hang out in Faith's room. If Faith shows up at the shelter, the others might get suspicious that such a good friend lives next door. So Allie "goes out for some air" by the front door, walks around the block and cuts through another neighbour's side-yard so she can knock on Faith's back door undetected. "See you then," Faith answers.

Faith manages to hammer out answers to five more questions on the SoulMate app before Allie arrives.

"I need your help," Faith says when Allie slips in the door.

"Who's that?" Bitta yells from the living room. The TV is blaring. She and her man friend (Faith refuses to say boyfriend or partner) have been shout-talking over the news rather than turning down the volume and speaking like civilized people.

"Hi, Mrs. Cooper!" Allie yells back.

"Oh, Allie!" Bitta exclaims, shuffling as quickly as she can to the back door before they can sneak into Faith's room. "Tell your best friend to finish that app profile *tout suite*."

"I did five more questions just now, Bitta," Faith says, shooting Allie an apologetic look.

"You should have the whole thing done by now," Bitta scolds. "Matthew is all ready to move in 13 days. He's none too happy I even offered the extra week."

"What app profile?" Allie asks.

"I know, I know," Faith says to Bitta, taking Allie by the elbow and ushering her into her room.

"You don't have time to fraternize…" Bitta is saying as Faith closes the door as gently as possible, crossing her fingers the closed door will spare her more ranting.

The two of them lean against the closed door, holding their breath, as Bitta utters more warnings. The passion increases but thankfully the volume does not and Faith breathes a sigh of relief once it is clear they have been left in peace. For now.

"What app profile?" Allie asks again.

"OMG," Faith drops onto the bed, "I need your help."

Allie sits down beside her and waits, eyebrows raised, looking put-together as usual with Pink Uggs to match her Canada

Goose coat. She sheds her coat and boots as Faith talks, settling on the bed beside her, facing the ceiling.

"I have thirteen days, Allie – *thirteen* – to find a job! I get a week more if I do this stupid SoulMate thing, but…"

"You're on SoulMate?! And you're just now telling me?" Allie shoves Faith in mock anger. "Everyone at the office is on that app and guess what? They've all coupled successfully!"

"Get out."

"Truth. If you want to find your soulmate, that's the way to do it," Allie says. "Wait, are you looking for your soulmate? I thought you were going to get yourself established first."

"I'm not against the idea, I have to admit," Faith says. "But yeah, the establishment part is stressing me out too." Faith pulls up the calendar on her phone. "Look, I have to be out by Nov. 30th. December 7th if I manage to get a miracle soulmate date by then…"

Allie cringes. "November and December aren't great hiring months. Unless you want retail."

"Yeah. I know! That's why I need help. You are way more organized than I am. Where do I begin?" Faith asks, a sting of tears threatening her eyeballs.

"Okay. You can do this," Allie says, placing her hand on Faith's arm. "First, breathe."

Faith forces herself to take five long breaths, the inhales and exhales growing longer with each repetition. It works. The tears are at bay. The fist around her stomach unclenches. "Now what?"

"Now you finish the app profile…" Before Faith can panic again, Allie says, "I will help you." She softens her voice, treading carefully. "Do you have any interviews coming up?"

"No!" Faith cries. She leaps off the bed and brandishes a week's worth of the newspaper's Jobs sections at Allie. Then she shows Allie the list of jobs she's applied for online, with all known rejections deleted.

"Okay, okay, then we will find some jobs to apply for together and I can come over, every day if you want, to update your to-do's. Sound good?"

Faith throws her arms around Allie and mumbles a tearful thank you into her perfectly straight hair. "You are the best. Absolutely the best!" she says.

"I know," Allie says, laughing. "What's the next app question?"

4
BRIAN

2. In what way would you like to be famous, if at all?

Zero desire to be famous.|

Too many haters, Brian thinks, after typing his answer. The world is too critical. Why open yourself up to that kind of abuse if you can avoid it?

Then again, he admits, after some consideration, he wouldn't mind being famous as an author. But not in a James Patterson kind of way. He would consider fame from publishing a quality book, a classic that professors assign as required reading. But he would have to be famous without the book-signings and interviews. If he couldn't be a live-in-the-woods hermit type of famous, where he could struggle to write something else in peace while being comforted that writing something else is unnecessary because he can die knowing he wrote one excellent book, then he'd rather not be famous at all. There would have to be a way to keep his flaws to himself, out of the public eye, play it safe, give up the glory for the sustained sense of accomplishment. That's the only type of famous he could consider.

He previews the next question, waiting for Tanica to shower and dress. Her outburst was not unusual. But he is unusually interested in pressing her for an answer this time.

A year ago when he discovered her cheating on him with a client, she denied it at first. When he confessed that Vivia saw them at an intimate dinner together, she said there's nothing wrong with having dinner with a friend. And when Jenson did some unauthorized investigative research on his own and stormed into her salon, slapping the damning photos onto the massage table that she was preparing for a wax client, their relationship barely recovered. Tanica was angry and vindictive, then remorseful and pleading. She said it was a one-time thing and wouldn't happen again. Brian agreed to trust her. But that was before he got *oblivious* stuck in his head.

Tanica blows off his innocent questions about her work and her social affairs as being controlling and in violation of his agreement to trust her. He buys into it, mostly because he doesn't want to know. Doesn't want to relive that torrential nightmare again. Trusting is so much easier than opening your eyes. But what has he done wrong, really? Why is he the controlling, suspicious one for wanting to know more about her life? He decides he will wait her out this time. He will cancel meetings if he has to, but he will stay right where he is until she comes down the stairs and answers his question.

The morning goes by quickly. He cancels a 2 o'clock meeting and reschedules a 3 o'clock interview and makes himself lunch. Then he pulls together enough research to write a convincing story on the medical virtues of cannabis, submitting it by the 4 o'clock deadline. He spends another hour finishing the Soul-Mate app questionnaire. He reviews it quickly, then presses enter before he can change his mind.

She finally walks down the stairs at 5:30. She stands at the bottom in her high red heels and short black skirt, rocking a low-cut striped blouse like always. Brian stays focused. Tanica seems surprised he is still there. He knows she was likely listening for the garage door to go up all day. "You have the day off, honey?" she says, like nothing happened.

How easy it would be for him to say, yes, *I thought I told you,* and allow her strange outburst to disappear into the past. Into oblivion, he thinks. But he fights the urge to keep the peace. "I rearranged some meetings, actually," Brian says. "Did you have a day off from the salon?"

A flicker of rage seems to light up her face in a nanosecond then disappears into her smile just as quickly; the smile reaching her eyes this time, giving the impression she is genuinely pleased that he is here, that they both have time off work, that they can do something together. "Also rearranged," she says. "I wish I knew, darling. We could have made a day of it." She walks over to him tentatively, where he sits in the same chair he has been all day, where she left him so dramatically at breakfast. "I have a 6 o'clock, though, so I'd best be off," she says, giving him a lingering kiss on the lips, pausing briefly to take in his eyes, knowing he won't be able to take them off her cleavage.

"Wax or hair?" he asks, as she turns away.

"What?" she says.

"Your 6 o'clock. Is it a wax or a hair client?"

"Oh," she says, with a nervous giggle. "Neither. Need to meet with the other gals to reconcile the books."

Before she can turn again, he says, "And last night. Where were you last night? I never got an answer to my question."

"If you must know," she says, "I was shopping for your birthday."

5
FAITH

3. What would prompt you to rehearse what you are going to say, before making a telephone call?

Okay full confession. I once ended up in a study group with a crazy hot guy. I mean, "couldn't look him in the eye for fear he would see my unbridled attraction to him written all over my face" hot. Every time I opened my mouth, nonsense came out. Pure nonsense. The others in the group looked at me like I'd grown four heads. Needless to say, I will definitely rehearse before study groups containing crazy hot guys. Phone calls though? Who calls anymore? That's why texting was invented.|

Faith had set her alarm an hour early so she could get a jump on the day. She and Allie finished the questionnaire for Soul-Mate and clicked enter together. What a load off that was! Before her alarm went off, she stared at her closed door for several minutes, mentally willing her grandmother to open it and start ranting about the app. Bitta must have a sixth sense about her when she's on top of things, because her door is still undisturbed.

She says good morning to Jasper and sprinkles seeds in his little gerbil dining area before he has a chance to stretch out of his hole and preen.

Next, she checks the giant calendar taped above her bed, where she and Allie entered in her daily tasks. She puts an X over yesterday, noting 19 days to find a job (not 12 since she signed up for SoulMate). Today's task: the fancy Toronto job "Wine Social Club Steward," and follow up with the Niagara-On-The-Lake winery retail clerk job, where she submitted her CV weeks ago, and for which no official rejection was issued. "Sometimes CVs get lost, or hiring managers get busy, any number of things," Allie had explained to her. "Always follow up."

Faith has allotted 25 minutes for each task. She opens her laptop, resists the urge to Google random thoughts, and completes both tasks in 30 minutes. She has time in the bank, she realizes. "Today might be a blow-dry day," she tells herself with pride.

Before she closes her laptop, she refreshes email just in case there is a quick reply from the two job options. No such luck. There is an email from SoulMate though. Must be an authentication email, she decides. It was well past business hours when she and Allie submitted her profile. She clicks on it since she has time. Need to keep that buy-an-extra-week-rent-free ball rolling.

Greetings, Faith!

Thank you for your SoulMate application. We are pleased to report you have a match living in your area. Once payment is remitted by both you and your match, one of you will be randomly selected to propose a first date time and location. See below for payment details. Of course, your payment will be refunded if you are unsatisfied...

Wow, that was fast, Faith thinks. Seems unlikely though. There must be a catch. She checks her bank account online and sees she can afford the SoulMate fee this week. For now. Until she has to pay rent somewhere. Or travel further than Montreal for an interview. She issues a payment from her account and tries to think positively.

She hears Jasper scratching at the side of his cage. She opens the top and scoops him up. He cocks his head at her. She kisses his little nose. "Things might just be working out for me, Jasper," she says. His little pink nose sniffs the air in wonderment. She sets him back in his cage and gives him half a peanut. She wonders who it was who dropped Jasper off at the Humane Society as a rejected pet. She tries to send a telepathic thank you to whoever performed this small but large act. It warms her heart to see sweet little Jasper scamper off to enjoy his peanut so eagerly.

6
BRIAN

3. What would prompt you to rehearse what you are going to say, before making a telephone call?

Rehearsing just makes things worse.|

B rian thinks about the first time he called a girl. She had a cute button nose and fly-away hair she rarely wore loose. They were both in Debate Club at school, so they knew how to put sentences together under pressure. But he soon learned that making well-researched policy arguments versus speaking to a real live person about weather, student council, and/or whether a person is interested in a date are two entirely different things. He didn't think he'd need to, but to ensure success, he rehearsed the phone call. He stood in front of his bathroom mirror every morning for a week, asking himself how the semester is going, does he like fall as much as summer, who does he think will be class president next year, and if she's free this Saturday, would she be interested in joining him for a movie. Yet when push came to shove, he tanked. He couldn't utter a single word after her melodic voice formed the sounds "hello" so effortlessly. He hasn't rehearsed a phone call since.

In fact, he and Tanica fell into easy conversation the minute they met at the salon. He was growing a beard for the first time and wasn't sure the barber was giving it quite the attention necessary. Jensen recommended Tanica's salon. The two of them talked non-stop through the whole appointment. Turns out he needed the right tools to do an effective beard-trimming job. He smiles, remembering the white hot attraction they had for each other. She was sleeping over regularly by date number three.

"There you are," Tanica says. He stands in front of the en-suite mirror, trimming his beard. After she explained her "surprise" birthday plans for him, he felt terrible. He said sorry he overreacted. She said sorry she is so bad at thinking up white lies on the spot. Then they made passionate love, just like they used to, right there in the living room. She was a little late to her meeting. He made her seared scallop frisée and opened the perfect bottle of Pinot Noir when she got home.

"I'm off to work. I'll be home by six," she says. Ah yes, they agreed to share schedules to prevent misunderstandings. How civilized.

"Great," Brian says. I'll be here." She kisses him on the neck. He wipes a bit of shaving gel off the tip of her nose.

"Oh," she says. "Two things."

He runs the razor carefully around his Adam's apple, raising his eyebrows to show he is listening.

"You caught a chipmunk."

He rinses his razor, laughing. "That little bugger has been riddling the flower garden with holes all summer. And we catch him in the winter? Amazing!"

"Yes, well, I don't know where you can release him. It's snowing. And supposed to get colder today."

"I'll think of something," he says. "What's the other thing?"

"Hmm?" she says, checking her blood red lipstick in the mirror. "Oh, your mother rang. She says she hasn't seen you in a while."

His mother lives in a separate apartment attached to their house. After his dad died, she agreed to relocate there so he could keep an eye on her. But she hasn't needed much looking after. Sometimes he thinks he saw her more often when she lived on the other side of town.

He rinses his face and towels off the residue. "Did she seem all right?"

Tanica grabs her purse off the bed and heads out the door. "Right as rain."

7
FAITH

4. What would constitute a "perfect" day for you?

I'm offered the perfect wine job. Ideally, export manager. But wine buyer is a close second. Also LCBO clerk. Also anything besides cashier at Farm Boy. Oh, and I meet my soulmate, we fall in love, and live happily ever after. And one more thing: animal rescuing. Lots of animal rescuing.

P.S. If I have to move for my dream job, my best friend moves too. P.S.S. And my soulmate has one of those jobs where he can live anywhere.

The end. That's my perfect day. Except for the fact that happily ever after part will take more than one day. Thank you. The End.|

F aith arrives at work 30 minutes early and is taking her time assessing the wine shipments when Stella walks into the stockroom, agitated.

"What happened to fall?" she says, more of a statement than a question as she peels off her feather-stuffed layers and fleece. "Car wouldn't start, Ralph useless this morning, had to take the bus, and the winter wear is still in basement bins, so that put me behind schedule, couldn't find any proper mitts, my fingers are icicles…" She continues her rant through the whole disrobing, boot-stomping, card-punching process.

Meanwhile, Faith spots a box of wine in the back of the night shipment stacks. She hasn't seen this one before. It's from SpringSide Winery, which happens to be the winery to which she drafted the follow-up email this morning. She picks up the box and carries it around the tower of hot house tomato boxes, all smiles, until she nearly bumps into Stella.

"Oh, hey there, Stella. Sorry your day is off to a bad start." She tries to frown in sympathy but in truth she feels invigorated by the clean, fresh snow-cover that painted her bus stop path this morning. And she is grateful for splurging on a sky blue puffy-coat last winter; one with a hood that kept her cozy all the way to work. When she passed by the foyer mirror on the way out of the house, she noticed the coat's colour makes her eyes stand out. She doesn't have many notable features, but her blue eyes have been a selling point in the handful of dates she's had.

The stockroom is kept cool and is slow to heat when fall slams into winter so Faith is still wearing her puffy-coat when she bumps into Stella.

"You going to prom or something?" Stella says, scanning Faith up and down with wide eyes.

Faith puts the box down and does her best to check herself out without a mirror. "Why? What? Am I overdressed?" Her coat is unzipped, and she's wearing a sweater for the first time this season. It's a drab grey one but it picks up the grey flecks in her eyes at least. And it's super soft. Because of its plunging V-neck, she had to layer it over a tank top. The coral coloured one was the only clean tank she had. Maybe it's a bit too shiny for work?

"No," Stella says. "Yes," she says. "You just look different today."

Faith is puzzled at first and then remembers. "Oh, I had time to blow-dry!" She spins around to give Stella the full view. "Even the back," she says, smiling.

Stella stands still with her stunned face for a few seconds longer. "I guess that's it then," Stella says. "You should blow-dry more often. Definitely won't be needing that SoulMate App…"

"Hey, I finished my profile, Stella, and guess what? I have a match already! Isn't that insane? And he lives somewhere close, apparently."

Stella shakes her head slowly in wonderment. "Well, sunshine, that is good news. Good for you." She looks down at the wine box. "That a new kind?"

"Yeah," Faith says. "It's from SpringSide. One of those Niagara wineries that popped up a few years ago. I hear it's starting to churn out some quality Cabernet Franc. One of my favourite varietals, actually. So I'm pretty psyched to see it. Oh, and I put in a CV for a job there but never heard back."

Stella helps her cut through the tape so they can get a look at the bottles. The labels are a cheerful turquoise blue dotted with fluffy white clouds. There is a plump, smiling bumble bee in the round part of the "p" in Spring that pulls the whole design together.

Faith is disappointed when she sees the shipment contains only Pinot Noir. No Cab Franc. She has never understood the Pinot trend. To her, it is a thin, vapid, unremarkable wine. Like picking up a glass of cherry Kool-Aid on a hot day and discovering someone forgot the sugar. And cut the flavour in half. And left it on the counter too long.

"Well," Stella says. "You match the label."

Faith laughs. "Me and my puffy-coat could be their model."

"And the bee matches your hair too. Honestly, I didn't know your hair was blonde."

Faith wraps her finger around a wavy section near her face. "Yeah, the frizz factor makes it mousier."

"Morning, ma-ladies," Chad says, shaking off his snow-covered toque, as he drifts through the doors. "Whoa." He stops short in front of the time clock. "Do you have an interview today or something?"

Faith feels her cheeks warm a little with embarrassment. "Aw thanks, you two. You made my day!" She checks the time on her phone. She doesn't want to miss a chance to stock the wine before her shift starts. "No interviews yet, but I'm hoping soon," she adds, looking at her phone. Twenty minutes left. Perfect. She checks her email one last time and sees she has two new messages. One from SpringSide and one from someone named Brian.

8
BRIAN

4. What would constitute a "perfect" day for you?

I wake up to a beautiful woman in my bed who loves me as much as I love her. I go to work, and my boss congratulates me on the best story I've ever written, maybe even gives me a raise. And the day concludes with a seafood-inspired plate of various colours and textures to delight the palate with which I can share a well matched bottle of Pinot Noir with said woman.|

Brian wishes he had asked Tanica to relocate the chipmunk somewhere on her way to work. He feels itchy just thinking about getting close to it. He's never had a pet, having discovered at a young age he breaks out in hives near all manner of creatures — dogs, cats, rabbits, birds, hamsters... Ah, well, he can cover himself well, maybe wear a scarf over his face, and there's always Benadryl if all else fails.

He wipes water drops from the marble sink counter and admires the clean bright ensuite space. This house with its clean lines and large windows, not to mention the mother-in-law quarters where his mom lives now, hit all the right marks when he went house hunting after his dad died.

He has never been a fan of clutter. It makes him anxious. And although he has done quite well for a journalist in a competitive field, he got a substantial enough boost from the will to afford moving on from the cramped apartment he shared with Jensen.

He was surprised all the money was left to him at first, until he saw the one condition, that he hold half of it in trust for his mother, providing for her every need. His mother has never been the needy type, and he is grateful to have her close, but he misses his dad every day.

That reminds him to check on his mother. He gives her a call before he forgets.

"Is this my handsome son?" she says by way of answering instead of hello.

"Morning Mom. Are you okay? Tanica says you came around looking for me." Brian looks in the mirror and straightens the collar of his polo. He likes this one better than his others. It's grey with playful flecks of blue. His eyes seem to pop when he wears it. *I am a handsome dude,* he thinks to himself.

"She seemed a bit crusty," his mom says. "Is there trouble in paradise?"

Brian knows that's code for *I don't like that witch*, and *Have you given her marching orders yet?* "We had a little spat, Mom. It's all good. You two should have coffee or something sometime. I think you'd like her better once you get to know her."

"I'm sure that's true, honey. Any girl who makes you happy, I like. You know that. Tell her she can call me anytime for coffee," she says, somehow managing the perfect tone between genuine and sarcastic.

"Will do, Mom. But how are you? Sorry I've been so busy we haven't crossed paths."

"Oh, I'm doing fine, thank you. I've been volunteering at the church. Nice group of women my age over there. And they do interesting things – not just quilting and baking. I saw that new exhibit at the War Museum. It is fantastic. One series by a Syrian woman painter took my breath away. And we did that bowling thing with the smaller, lighter balls. I got the highest score, but there's a rematch tomorrow, loser buys shots at the bar. And that reminds me what I wanted to ask you…"

"What's that, Mom? And by the way, your life is a helluva lot more interesting than mine. How is that fair?"

She laughs. The bubbling pleasant laugh of an older woman who doesn't take herself too seriously. "I'll tell you the secret, Brian."

"Lots of booze," they say together and chuckle.

"Are you free tonight? I picked up some fresh shrimp from the market. Perfect for martini night."

"It's martini night, is it?" Brian says. His mother hosts her own private martini night once a week or so. It's her day off from cooking, a reward after she's cleaned her entire apartment. Usually pealed and cooked shrimp with cocktail sauce. Served with a perfect martini up with olives (the only vegetable allowed). Sometimes jarred mini onions end up in their martinis with the olives, if the movie she picks on Netflix is a long one.

"Oh yes, I'm scraping at the shower mold as we speak," she says, water slopping sounds in the back ground. "You can bring that Tanica girl."

Brian laughs. "I wouldn't miss it, Mom. Thanks for the invite. I'll let you know about Tanica."

"Wonderful," she says. "Bye now." She hangs up without giving him a time.

He shakes his head and sees he has a text. "Meeting moved up to 9AM," Jensen's text says. That's in 20 minutes. He checks his email, as he grabs a salmon-coloured sweater from his closet. He has a new message from SoulMate. That was fast. He takes a few more minutes to pay the fee from his work account before heading out the door.

9
FAITH

5. Would you prefer the mind or the body of a 30-year-old the last 60 years of your life?

So do I want a stellar figure, even when I'm 80? Or a stellar mind at 80? I mean, I've seen some 80-year-olds with decent minds and figures, but typically it seems their minds are slipping or their bodies are falling apart, or both. Oh my, can you even imagine an 80-year-old woman walking around with a stellar figure but no light on upstairs? I can only hope I'm as sharp as my grandmother is. That woman still attracts the men. In fact, she has a much younger one moving in with her soon. It's kind of gross but good for her. So to answer the question, I prefer the option of shooting for a 40ish-year-old-body AND mind until the bitter end. But if I have to choose? Like a genie is holding a gun to my head? I guess I pick mind. Because it's hard to appreciate a vain, figure-obsessed old lady, especially if she can't remember what she had for breakfast. And once you're old enough to have all that wisdom, well you should just own that wisdom and flaunt it like the figure you wish you had!

Stella was right. Faith should blow-dry more often. Every customer that she rings through seems to take longer than typical to chitchat and pay. Maybe it's her imagination, but the men especially linger a little too long, making eye contact most of the time, though she now realizes the tank may be a tad bit revealing at the V-line of her sweater. On break, she checked her wine display and decided the Pinot deserves an eye-level spot because of the label. She fought the urge to relegate it to the bottom shelf, finding it difficult to believe people really like that grape. But based on the sales from her cash register at least, it seems to be flying off the shelf.

She makes a dash to Starbucks, only a few stores away in the Farm Boy strip centre, but wow is it cold! She usually brings an apple or something portable and free for lunch, but today she is splurging a little to celebrate what feels like good fortune coming her way. She checks her phone as she waits in line for her almond pumpkin spice latte no whip, already imagining the feel of its papery smooth warmth cradled in her frozen fingers. She loves that Starbucks is the Burger King of coffees. "Have it your way," the green siren seems to say. "Do you want it grande or short? Cow milk or non-dairy? Fat or no fat? Sugar or no sugar? Do you want fries with that?" She has to laugh, as she enjoys the pre-PSL anticipation.

Before her shift, she saw that her potential soulmate has paid the fee (already!) and has been selected as the one to choose a meeting locale. She is curious where it will be. She imagines that place in the Glebe with steak and truffle-frites that pair perfectly with Cab Franc. She wonders if he pays or do they split the bill? Probably they split the bill, the first time, she thinks. In that case, maybe not the Glebe place. Faith's stomach grumbles, and she realizes she left the house without breakfast. Breakfast! Maybe they will go to that diner she likes. The affordable one that puts more than two vegetables in their omelet without charging extra.

She has two messages – the one from SpringSide she didn't have time to read and a new one from Brian. Interesting. She clicks on the Brian one first.

"Hi there 'soulmate,'" it says. Aw, that's cute. "Looking forward to meeting you. The gods have chosen me to select the place and time so hope you like Bridgehead. Is 3:00 today too soon? The one in the Glebe? See you soon, Brian."

OMG, Faith thinks. Today at 3:00? Bridgehead? I mean, they make a good cappuccino, but God help me if my soulmate is local indie-coffee obsessed.

The barista calls her name, and Faith smiles at the personal touch. Aw, he said Fate instead of Faith. That's kind of eerie considering I just heard from my soulmate, she thinks with a giggle. The PSL feels great in her hands, and she is happy she got one today so she won't be annoyed with Bridgehead. One time she went there with Bitta and her church friends. They were featuring a pumpkin-ginger latte, and she had to pour it out, it was so gross. She takes a small sip of her perfectly blended latte and feels her entire body vibrate with pleasure. What a day – she just so happens to look great, she feels great, and she has a date!

Before she heads back to Farm Boy (*I'll need to switch shifts with someone,* she realizes. *Better get a move on.*) she clicks on the SpringSide email, not even considering the potential rejection as something to prepare for mentally. Nothing is going to get her down today.

> Dear Ms. Cooper:
>
> Thank you for your follow-up message. Please accept my sincere apologies for the delay. We are understaffed and the hiring manager is off on maternity leave. We are indeed interested in speaking with you. I am afraid we cannot afford to pay your way from Ottawa to Niagara, but we do have a Wine Buyer in your area tomorrow. If you are still interested, please call or text him (contact info below) and set up a time to meet. Thank you for your patience.
>
> Samuel Smyth
> SpringSide Winery President

Faith almost spills her coffee when she jumps up and down at the "we are indeed interested part." And she barely feels the cold when she runs down the sidewalk back to Farm Boy.

10
BRIAN

5. Would you prefer the mind or the body of a 30-year-old the last 60 years of your life?

For my soulmate or for me? Just kidding. I suppose the politically correct answer is to preserve mind over physical. If all we have at the end of life is a great body, but not enough brains to contribute to the world, the world would be a sad place. Like a bunch of Donald Trumps walking around, except better looking. Still, it's tempting to choose body in that being fit enough to travel and try new activities would be ideal in later years where time seems shorter and shorter, and the world even more vast than it is in our youth. Despite the temptation to choose otherwise, I can honestly say I would choose mind. Even if I can't get around, I can at least keep writing. And the more I write the more likely I will leave the world with something worth reading.

Why is there no word limit on these questions? Mind. I pick mind!|

"Sorry I'm late," Brian says, walking into the conference room with a bag of Tim Hortons donuts and four coffees. "I guess winter's here now. Everyone's driving like they've never seen snow."

Sid, Jensen and Vivia, who already have mugs of office coffee, turn to look at the scene outside the window. "Apparently, the Mayor bought more snow plows," Jensen says. "I've never seen so many."

"Might be a story there," Sid says to Jensen, "you should check it out. See if tax increases tie into it." Sid Steele is the junior editor in charge of their little group. He seems to get heat when things don't run smoothly, so that's the only time they meet.

Vivia gets up and grabs one of the coffees. "Double double. Thanks Brian." Brian notices her mug is full and untouched.

"My svelte figure will not be thanking you for the doughnuts," Jensen says, powdered sugar on his lips, as he passes the box to Vivia. She selects the glazed chocolate cake kind as Brian predicted, and passes the box to Sid who waves them away.

"Thanks, Brian. Let me get straight to the point here," Sid says. Typical Sid, not much for the small talk. More about problem-solving than a people person. "The last article you submitted wasn't bad…"

"Thank you," Brian says, grabbing an apple fritter from the box and tearing off a juicy clump. "I see it got published, so that's good."

"Yes, it's been done before, the whole medical benefits angle, but you had an, um, interesting take on it. Thing is…" Sid glances at Vivia and Jensen, who become fascinated by their donuts at that moment. "...I was under the impression you would be submitting an investigative piece about that new dating app."

"SoulMate. Right. They told me," Brian says, trying to make eye contact with Jensen and failing that, Vivia, to discern where this is heading.

"And I see you did sign up for it. Finally. And charged it to the paper."

Brian freezes mid-bite. Sets the fritter globule down on the lid of his coffee. "That's right."

"I just need your assurance that this isn't going to be one of those goody two-shoes fluff pieces like Jensen writes..." Jensen widens his eyes in feigned offence. "...that it's an exposure story, not a feel good one. That's why we gave the story to you – the classic unbiased reporter with a bite that you are."

Brian can't hide his confusion, but then he gets it. "Oh, I see. You're worried I'll actually fall in love and bail on the story."

"Well," Sid says, "I can't stop a fellow from falling in love. But that can't be the story. The story is that there's something fishy about this app, it's obviously flawed, and you are the guy who figures it out."

Brian nods.

"You have figured it out, right?" Sid asks.

Brian clears his throat. "Well, the technology is patented, so there's little in the way of research. And I haven't actually gone on the date yet..." Sid opens his mouth to interrupt so Brian continues quickly. "...but the questionnaire process is unique. Obviously distracting and unscientific. It extracts the type of drivel you'd hear in a therapist's office." He notices a furtive glance between Jensen and Vivia. "I have *not* been to a therapist, but I can imagine. Anyway, I do not believe the app connects soulmates; I do not believe in the concept of soulmates, and the story I plan to write will likely take the position that the app is more about marketing and psychology, convincing people they have the real deal because it must be true if there's science behind it, not because they actually have anything in common. I mean, come on, research shows we can fall in love with anyone given the right circumstances…" And provided the right conversations occur in the beginning, he starts to add, and then doesn't. "…soulmates do not exist, 110%, and besides, I am happily in love with my own *soulmate…*" He uses air quotes for this. "…no chance I'll fall in love."

Nailed it, he thinks, and stuffs a giant piece of fritter in his mouth. The three watch him skeptically as he chews maniacally, like a kid in a candy shop.

"Good," Sid finally says. "When is the date?"

Brian checks his phone and sees the ball is in his court for setting up the date. "How is today at three?"

$$\frac{11}{\text{FAITH}}$$

6. Do you have a secret hunch about how you will die?

I thought about being funny or clever here, like hopefully in a barnyard full of furry creatures. Suddenly, let's hope. While drinking Cab Franc after a steak & frites lunch. But in case honesty drives this app, I don't have a secret hunch. My mother died too young of brain cancer, and she was a good person. My deadbeat dad is still kicking around somewhere, but he only cares about money and himself. So if I had to guess, my hunch is I will die at a reasonable age, possibly after kicking cancer's butt for a while, and fighting like hell to be a good person despite my inclination to focus too much on the conveniences money offers.|

Faith flies like a bat out of hell to get to Bridgehead on time and still manages to be late. She pauses only once, at the window between the bus stop and Whole Foods that is big enough and shadowed enough to reflect. She reassembles her frightful flight of hair, adds a little shimmer to her lips, the guava frost that people seem to notice when she wears it, and spritzes a little beach spray she borrowed from Stella to counteract any sweating that ensues from her rush and/or anxiety. She's meeting her soulmate. She can't believe it. Good thing she doesn't have time to focus on it.

She bursts through the Bridgehead doors, fully aware she will dominate the first moments of their first conversation with all the excuses she pondered on her flight over, and suddenly realizes she doesn't know what he looks like. There were no photos accompanying the SoulMate communications. Or the email from Brian himself. No last name to google. She has no idea what he looks like. Oh God. What if he's old? Or ugly? She never even thought of that. No matter. If their souls match, they match. Old or not. Ugly or not.

For now there is a bigger problem and that is, as she scans the booths, tables and hodgepodge of comfy chairs that are sprinkled with single-looking men, she has no idea which one he is. And how will he know it's her? She particularly hopes he doesn't think it's the girl on the comfy chair by the window. She's basically perfect. Thin, well dressed, pleasant expression, reading something on her laptop that makes her look smart, with the right mix of pensiveness and humour playing across her face. If he thinks it's her and then sees me... well, that's going to be a jolt.

"Hi." Faith nearly jumps out of her skin when a man comes up from behind and places his hand on her bicep. "Are you Faith?"

She wheels around and what she sees creates a whirl in her head that won't seem to stop. Is she still turning? Oh God, please say I'm not still turning in the middle of Bridgehead like a crazy person, she thinks.

"I'm looking for a woman named Faith," he says.

"Woman," she thinks. He was expecting a woman?

This guy is a hunk. Like tongue-stilling, choke-on-your-coffee, can't-function-for-fear-you'll-dim-his-bright-bright-light hunky. But is he old? She can't quite tell. Surely he wasn't expecting a woman.

Faith is suddenly aware she has failed to answer his question. How much time has gone by since he asked her name? Seconds? Minutes? Say something, she tells herself, answer him. Faith folds in her lips awkwardly to get them working. Hopefully, he's focused on the guava shimmer and not the oh-my-god-you're-ugly impression her compressed lips must be giving. "You're NOT ugly," she blurts out, too loudly, too shrilly. How many people just turned and scowled at her disapprovingly, she wonders. Two? Three? *Oh my God, did I just say "you're not ugly" in answer to his "are you Faith" question?*

Come on, Faith, you can do this, she thinks. *Just activate brain and move lips. It's not that hard. You do this every day.*

He's so tall, her brain says. Imagine him cocking his head just a little and planting a kiss on you right now. He is just the right kind of tall to pull that move off perfectly. And that beard. She imagines the bristly softness of it forming a little nest around her mouth as she stands on tip-toe to meet his kiss. She can feel her nose tingle in anticipation of his beard brushing against it, light as a feather, like a faint tickle…

Faith shakes her head. Activate brain, she chides herself. Not hormones. Brain. In fact, hormones, you stay out of this for a while. I need to think.

Wait. Why isn't he saying anything? I mean clearly I'm paralyzed from the neck up right now and lack all social graces as far as he can discern by this point. But he seems to be staring into my soul. (Which isn't fair because he's using his obvious powers of handsomeness to magically disarm me.) And he's not saying anything.

All this plays out in Faith's head in a matter of seconds that stretch into what she considers to be at least an hour before she finally utters, in a somewhat normal tone of voice, the most clever thing she can think of.

"My name is Faith." Okay, it's a start, she thinks.

12
BRIAN

6. Do you have a secret hunch about how you will die?

I mean, that's kind of a lame question, isn't it? Morbid and trite. Not a great combo. But if I'm given a last supper like a man on death row, I'm definitely going with burger and fries. And a good bottle of Pinot. Because it seems to pair well with everything. The "good" bottles, anyway. If all goes well and my death follows a genetic path rather than a tragic one, I hope I have my mother's genes. She somehow seems to get younger as she ages. However she goes, she will have lived a full, happy life. She outlived Dad. A heart attack caught him by surprise. But he lived a full, happy life too and if he were here now, he wouldn't change a thing about his lifestyle. He and Mom had a lot of fun. Good people.

So once again, there really should be word limits on these answers. No hunch is my answer.|

B etween the meeting and his date, Brian managed to find a former employee of the SoulMate company, who was willing to talk to him off the record. The fellow probably had to sign a confidentiality agreement to work there. Still, there might be something he can use or a lead he can follow after he meets with this guy.

The newspaper offices are centrally located, with an easy 20 minute walk to Bridgehead. Tanica's salon is on the way. He decides to stop by there since he has some extra time. The place is buzzing and it takes the receptionist a long time to notice him between answering the phone, fetching product for this stylist and that, and leading foil-headed women from the dryers to the shampoo sinks. When he is finally able to inquire about Tanica, he is told she left an hour ago. "For the day?" he asks.

"That's right," the receptionist says. "She booked the rest of the day off."

Wonderful, Brian thinks. He'll get this date over with, then be home with lots of time to butter Tanica up. He knows she and Mom will get along once they get to know each other, and martini night is an ideal opportunity for girl bonding, from his experience.

When he arrives at Bridgehead, Brian realizes he has no way to identify this Faith person. He takes out his phone and makes a note about that. More evidence of a flawed system. No photo. No last name. He supposes he could have asked her in the email, so maybe that's on him. Still, why a popular app would fail to provide identifying information, relieving the couple of any axe-murder related fears, defies logic.

He glances around the place and wonders if he should have chosen a quieter Bridgehead. He doesn't see any open seats. All the single-looking women in the place are more preoccupied with their screens or companions than they are with their environment, so he is able to check them off the list one by one as they fail to look up in search of this much anticipated date.

A few minutes go by, and he starts to wonder if he gave Faith the wrong time or location. He pulls up his sent emails to check. No. He was very clear. Glebe Bridgehead. 3:00.

Just as he places the phone back into his Canada Goose jacket pocket, a young lady bursts through the doors and frantically scans the place. He is behind her, closer to the alcove surrounding the doors where he retreated to check his phone. And she seems to be dwelling longer than necessary on the single-looking men, as she scans the room. He suspects she might be the one. A blond, he notices by the back of her head. And young, judging by her herky-jerky actions. He automatically pictures the girl from the pub. Not too bright. Not his type. If she drinks wine at all, it's pink and only when she has to buy her own. It occurs to him he will have to hurt her feelings and feels no pride in that thought.

He takes a step toward her tentatively. He doesn't want to scare her. He taps her on the arm, seems like the safest least offensive place to touch her before they've met, and says hi. "Are you Faith?"

Oops, he did scare her. She jumps and spins around. He doesn't want to frighten her more, or get punched in the face for assault so he quickly blurts out, "I'm looking for a woman named Faith."

Just as he is about to hold his hands up in surrender, to fend off any punches and also signify his innocence, the world goes fuzzy. People in the coffeeshop seem to move in slow motion. There is an intense buzzing in his ears, masking the conversations around him. He wonders if he is having a heart attack or a panic attack because the only vision he has is of her, only her. Like she's standing in a spot light on a dark stage. All while he shrinks away until it seems he is seeing her from some skyward place far above.

He wills his hands to move. If he can touch his face, feel for his mouth to see if it's still there, he can determine if he's alive or if he's in a dream.

And just as he imagines death might be, he is able to take in all her features and mannerisms in what must be a short amount of time but seems like hours. Her eyes. Bright with innocence and whimsy. The delicate wave of hair that frames her face and stretches toward her chest just past her ballerina-like shoulders. There are exactly five freckles around her nose. He has time to count them all. Three on her left and two on her right. The colour and pattern of her irises illogically match his own. A cerulean blue with flecks of grey on the edges, the same colour grey as her sweater. He has time to take in her undershirt from which her shapely breasts peek out in just the right way – sexy but not showy. He hopes she doesn't see him linger on her chest but if he could form a sentence he would tell her it is a beautiful chest but the rest of her is more beautiful. Actually, he thinks there is no "more." She is the entire package and he never imagined such a package could exist.

He is painfully aware he hesitated too long. He's been silent all this time, mannerless. It is clear to Brian he is not in fact dead, so he must be dumbstruck. And she has had too long to form exactly the worst possible first impression of him. First impressions are the most powerful. He knows that. And he blew his chance to impress her. He suddenly feels hideous in her presence. Not only is he a fraud who showed up intending to hurt her, but he is a hairy old mess of an ogre standing before a goddess.

Before he can verbalize his apology and escape (But oh must he escape? He would give anything to linger here with her just a little longer.), she says, "You're not ugly." And just like that, Brian is set at ease. His lips are freed, and he is able to form the words necessary to demonstrate his humanity. She confirms she is the Faith he is looking for, and he lets this news sink in. She didn't run away. She didn't punch him in the face. She is still here.

"I'm not ugly," he manages to parrot back.

She laughs, and it is a beautiful, melodic laugh. Her freckles darken as the skin around them deepens to a rosy blush. "That is not the first sentence I intended to say to you," she finally says. They laugh together then. She, laughing good-naturedly at herself. Brian, laughing with relief: she mistook his parroted remark as calculated cleverness. Thank God.

"Oh look," she says, pointing at the window alcove, "some seats opened up."

Brian spots the chairs she means and is relieved they are the high backed comfortable ones. Sitting on one of those low stools or deep booth seats would have been awkward. Together they claim the chair with their jackets and move toward the bar.

"I've got this," Brian says. "What do you like?"

He can tell she is pleased rather than offended by chivalry, which is good. He's making progress here. She squints at the menu, wrinkling her freckled nose, "I don't know," she says somewhat nervously. "What are you having?"

"They make a good cappuccino here," he says.

"Great, I'll have that."

He goes to the end of the line. She heads back to the chairs but turns around last minute and asks, "Do they have almond milk?"

"I'll ask," he says. "If they don't, do you want to change your order?"

"No," she says. "That's okay. I'll…" The cute crinkled squint at the menu again. "I'll have it however you take it."

Once the cappuccinos are made, Brian and Faith settle into the window chairs. Curious, Brian asks, "Do you have a lactose intolerance?"

"No," she says. "Not that I know of, anyway. It's just something new I'm trying lately. Almond milk instead of cow's milk."

"Vegan then?"

"God no. I'd die a slow death if I couldn't eat steak ever again."

They both laugh at that. "No allergies, then. Check." He draws a check-mark in the air, smiling.

There is an awkward pause. Then she says, "How about you? Allergies? Menu restrictions? *Food* issues?" she says, with air quotes around food.

"No, I eat anything," he says. "I'm allergic to pets though," he adds with a laugh.

She seems a bit concerned for him, like a mother worrying over a child's sneeze, he thinks. That's kind of cute. "What kind of pets?" she asks.

"All manner of pets."

She doesn't respond so he fills the silence with useless banter about his job, his mother (she seems surprised she lives with him), his friends, his work on the cannabis policies (she has read some of his articles and seems impressed). He stops himself from talking about his current project when he realizes it involves possibly hurting her (although he is honestly starting to question whether he could go through with that, he already likes her so much), so he changes the subject to wine. When he mentions Pinot, her nose crinkles again, but not in a good way, like a wince. "You don't like Pinot?" he asks, trying to appear impartial about it.

"It's devoid of all the qualities I treasure in wine," she replies. "It's limp, vapid, anemic and tasteless."

He shudders.

She sees it. "I'm sorry," she says. "I know it's very popular. I'm a sommelier, actually, so of all people, I should be the one going on about Pinot right now, right? But I just don't get it."

Brian stiffens. "You're a sommelier, and you can't appreciate Pinot Noir?"

Her smile fades. "Hoo boy, I've really stepped into now, haven't I?" She tugs at her sweater, starts to sip her coffee, then puts the cup down.

Speaking fast, she brings up her hobby of rescuing gerbils. She rattles on and on about how cute they are and smart. Kissable. (Kissable! He feels sick just thinking about it.) Easy to take care of and surprisingly abandoned quite often when parents cave to the pleading of their children too young to care for them… Brian tries to mask his lack of interest and in doing so realizes he forgot about the chipmunk.

Her going on about rodents like they are charming little nymphs while he likely has a frozen rodent corpse on his back patio seems desperately funny to him all of the sudden. He tries to stifle the chuckle bubbling up inside him, but he can't. With all the nerves and wine talk and craziness, his emotions are wound so tight, the release of laughter is just too strong. His chuckle becomes a childish giggle, the giggle evolves into a full on belly laugh, and before he can will himself to take back some control, there are tears streaming down his face and he is forced to bend over, like he's been sucker-punched, to quell the laughter-induced pain in his stomach.

"I'm sorry," he manages to breathe out in rapid, gasping bursts. "You've just reminded me," and the laughter starts up again, "that I've managed to kill a creature today you might have loved." And as the words he just sputtered carelessly between breaths reform themselves in his mind, he realizes he has no chance with this girl whatsoever.

13
FAITH

7. What three things are most important to have in common with your partner?

Attraction is crucial, I believe. I know there are stories of couples being friends and "growing" to love each other, but I can't help thinking that's more like settling than love. Passion fades, but if it's not there to begin with that's a red flag for me. Sex should be good too, I suppose. I haven't actually gone "all the way," but I've done enough to get that parts should be somewhat complimentary in nature, and partners should be in tune enough with each other to hit all the right buttons, so to speak. So yeah. Let's see, what else? Animals! He should respect animals as much as I do, even if he isn't passionate about them. So there you have it:

Attraction

Sex

Respect for Animals|

14
BRIAN

7. What three things are most important to have in common with your partner?

Attraction

Good sex

Must love Pinot Noir. (Ha, ha, just kidding.) (Seriously though.)|

15
FAITH

8. For what in your life do you feel most grateful?

It's a toss-up so I'm going to go ahead and cheat on this question, so if that gets my application tossed in the trash, so be it. I'm most grateful for my best friend, Allie, without whom I literally would not be able to complete this questionnaire without a thousand ADD moments. Also, she saved me years of therapy by taking me under her wing when I most needed a wing to be under back in high school. I am also equally most grateful for my grandmother, without whom I would be literally on the streets right now. She also paid for my business and wine program courses. I hate to think how deep in debt I'd be or how many fast food restaurants I'd be working at if she had not done that for me. Also, I love her so much. She's a tough old bag, but only because she knows how tough it is out in the real world.|

Faith wakes up with a start. Only 18 more days until she is out on the street. That's seven days more than she could have had, thanks to that app business happening so quickly, but if she's going to avoid the streets, and let's face it, if she's going to have a life at all, she needs to stay focused.

She hops up on to her feet, and scratches another giant X over yesterday on the calendar. She considers her progress. She got a date. It could have gone better, but at least she got a date. And she has an interview today. The wine buyer from SpringSide seemed nice on the phone. He has an old name but a young voice. She writes on today's calendar slot "10 AM Interview with Morty Richmond."

She scans her to do list. No word yet from the fancy wine place in Toronto. So all she has to do is apply for two more positions. She can do that after work.

And she can't forget she works the afternoon shift today. She had to take Angela's shift to get coverage for yesterday. "WORK: 3:00 she writes on the calendar" below "Interview."

She is dying to talk to Allie, so she texts her now to see if she's left for work yet. "I have 30 minutes," Allie texts back. Excellent. That will leave Faith time to shower and blow-dry appropriately before her Interview.

She barely has a chance to feed Jasper when she hears Allie's knocking. She races to the door.

"Who is it?" Bitta shouts from the living room. Before Allie can answer, Bitta is right there with her, lightning fast for Bitta, to greet Allie.

"Did she tell you about the soulmate?" Bitta asks Allie.

"He has a name," Faith says.

"Hi Mrs. C.," Allie says, "No, I had to work late last night. Big trial happening today. You should see the exhibit room!" She spreads her arms as wide as she can to demonstrate. "How'd it go?" She grabs her hand and pretends to scrutinize it. "I don't see a ring on your finger."

Faith giggles.

"Oh, she's not that easy," Bitta says. "She's got to have at least three dates before he gets in her pants."

"Bitta!" Faith says, horrified.

Bitta looks at her severely. "It's a rule. I'm not kidding." She gives Allie a little hug. "Okay you've talked to this old lady long enough. Go do your catching up," she says, and saunters off down the hall.

"There's not much time so dish," Allie says excitedly, once they're both on the bed, knees touching, crisscross style. "Is he gorgeous? Tell me he's gorgeous."

Faith opens her mouth to answer.

"Is he rich? Tell me he's rich."

Faith appears to think about this one.

"Does he have a friend? Tell me he has a friend."

"Okay, can I get a word in edgewise here?" Faith says.

"You're right, you're right, sorry," Allie says. She makes a sweeping gesture with her arm. "Please continue." She folds up her lips and pretends to lock them with a key.

"First of all," Faith begins, "yes, he's gorgeous." Allie squeals, then puts her hand over her mouth, eyes wide. "I don't know if he's rich, but he does the political reporting for the paper, so he can't be doing too badly."

"He's a–?" Faith shoots her a warning look and Allie puts her hand over her mouth again.

"We didn't talk about friends. In fact, now that I think about it, he didn't ask much about me. But here's the thing."

Allie's mouth is still covered, her eyes couldn't be wider.

"We seemed to hit it off huge at first. I mean. He's tall and bearded and blue-eyed and when he looks at you he looks straight into your soul. It would be creepy if it weren't so hot."

Another squeal from Allie.

"And I'm pretty sure he was into me too."

Allie's brows furrow at the word "was."

"But things kind of fizzled when I pushed for almond milk in my cappuccino."

Allie glares at Faith scoldingly.

"What, he picked Bridgehead! I've got nothing when I look at that menu. No pumpkin spice, no toffee-nut, no…"

Faith nods sympathetically and gestures for her to get on with it.

"And more fizzling occurred when I mentioned I hate Pinot, which he looooves," Faith rolls her eyes.

Allie's shoulders slump.

"And the fizzle of all fizzles? He had a huge laughing fit over killing a chipmunk after I blabbered nonstop about gerbil love."

Here their shoulders slump simultaneously.

After a moment of silence, Faith says, "You can talk now."

"How did you leave things?" Allie asks, her tone the total opposite of a squeal. "Is there any hope?"

"I don't know. We kind of talked about weather and shit like that for a while, trying to act like it's all good, but after the coffee was gone, we made excuses for needing to get on with the next item on our itineraries. He said it was nice meeting me."

"Nice?" Allie says, making her hand into a gun and mock shooting herself in the head.

"And he shook my hand."

Allie collapses onto the bed like she's dead, and Faith lays down beside her. They stare at the spitball stains on the ceiling for a while (That was a fun sleepover, Faith recalls).

"Do you still get the extra week?" Allie asks.

"Totally," Faith says, grateful for the silver lining.

"Okay then. You know what you've got to do, right? Keep to the schedule."

Faith smiles and squeezes Allie's hand. "I will. I'm applying for two more jobs today. Oh!" she exclaims, "I nearly forgot. I have an interview this morning with that Niagara winery you convinced me to follow up on. Here in town though. This morning!"

"Now that's what I wanted to hear," Allie says. "Way to go, girl. Kill it!"

16
BRIAN

8. For what in your life do you feel most grateful?

OK let's just keep this simple and state the obvious: Pinot Noir|

Brian decides to walk all the way home from Bridgehead. He needs the 30 minutes to process what just happened so he can focus on quality time with Tanica. He remembers it's martini night, which cheers him. Two things to look forward to.

Meeting with Faith caused a whirlwind of emotion he had not experienced in some time. Maybe not ever. It was frightening, now that he thinks about it. The opposite of what he has with Tanica. But what he experienced was more than lust. Faith was attractive, yes, but her mere presence stopped him in his tracks. He couldn't speak. Is that normal?

He thinks back to when he first met Tanica. The camaraderie they shared from the start. That seems normal to him. That's a sensible start to a relationship. Was he that attracted to her from the start? Yeah he was attracted. She's a beautiful woman. But it was a different type of attraction with Tanica. More primal somehow.

What would he call the attraction he had for Faith, he wonders. If not primal, what? The buzzing and the blurring and the out of body experience comes rushing back to him when he thinks of his first reaction to her. That was just. Well, the only thing he can think of that comes close is smoking weed.

Brian shakes his head. This isn't helpful. Every relationship is different. This was just what "another" relationship might look like if he were open to one beyond Tanica. Which he's not, he reassures himself.

He's attracted to women all the time. He is a man after all. That doesn't make it a threat to what he has with Faith. Tanica, he meant. *Oblivious.* Okay enough on that. *Focus. Be aware.* He is well aware now that feelings for other women can be intense. He'll need to tread carefully the next time he experiences something like that. That's all. Just be careful.

Besides, he tells himself. Faith hates Pinot Noir. Some sommelier. And then there was that almond milk conversation. He's never enjoyed people with high maintenance food qualms.

Oh and the gerbil thing. Well, that could just never happen. If they did have some *soulmate* type connection (He says it sarcastically in his head.), they could never be together. She would have to give up gerbils. Or he would have to drink Benadryl for

77

breakfast every day. Not happening. He does feel a little guilty about accidentally freezing the chipmunk. He doesn't like holes in his garden, but he never meant to kill the poor little guy. Okay then, so that's that.

So in the morning he will draft an email to SoulMate describing how much of a bust the date was. See how long it takes them to return his money. The paper's money.

After that he meets with the ex-employee. See if that leads anywhere. He should have an article for Sid within the next two days.

He chuckles, thinking how weak the app is. How many times did he write on the questionnaire how much he likes Pinot Noir? *But did she write on hers that she doesn't like it?* Not much point focusing on that.

He mentally checks off the list of things to process as his house comes into view. Faith. Over and done with. SoulMate article. In the hamper after tomorrow's interview. Oh, and the last thing, he realizes, is to dispose of the chipmunk.

He'd like to think Tanica has done it already, having been home half the day. He could always call in a birthday favour since his 30th is looming large. Well, he'll have to see what kind of mood she's in when he gets home.

17
FAITH

9. If you could change anything about how you were raised, what would it be?

For starters, I'd like my mother back. I had Allie in my corner during the potentially rebellious years, but had Mom been there, I'd be in the process of growing closer to her now. Grandma's advice is great, but Mom had a softer touch. And a little brother would have been nice. A big brother would have been better. Someone I could ask advice about guys and get the true blue scoop. Other than that, I think Mom did a stellar job raising me. I have no complaints. My grandmother? She'd say my Mom was too soft.|

F aith meets Morty from SpringSide at an art gallery in the Byward Market. He is hosting a function there for restaurant owners, sommeliers, and valued clients who buy wine. The ones who have bought from SpringSide before are even more important, he tells her. The whole affair feels more like a fun learning experience than an interview.

"How did you find the sommelier program?" he asks while they set up glasses and organize winery placards on the various tables invitees will visit.

"It was great. I learned a lot," Faith says. "I can identify a Cab Franc like nobody's business," she adds and he laughs.

"Where did you get your diploma?" she asks him.

"Queens," he says. He hands her a bottle and a wine key, gestures for her to open it.

"Really? I wasn't aware Queens has a sommelier program." Faith says. She navigates the bottle opening without a hitch, thanks to opening hundreds of bottles during her training. She sniffs the cork. "It's fine," she says. "Are you decanting this one?"

"No," he says. "Not enough decanters for all the quality bottles here." He points at the bottle still in her hands. "That one's $80 retail."

She almost drops it. Morty takes it out of her hands and carefully sets it on the Trius table, laughing. "I don't have a sommelier degree, by the way, I graduated with a degree in chemistry."

"Wow, that's impressive. You must know so much about, well the chemical makeup of wine, and that…kind of thing." *Come on Faith,* she tells herself. *Get it together.*

"Right," he says. Then laughs. "Don't tell anyone," he whispers conspiratorially, "but it's the best job I could find. If you're a lapsed pre-med student and you don't want to work in a lab, your choices are limited."

"Oh," she says. "I'm sorry the pre-med thing didn't work out."

"Don't be," he says. "Best thing that ever happened to me. I realize now I'm too much of a social creature to work in science. SpringSide is a great place to work. I think you'd get along well there."

"Thank you," Faith says, pleased that the Interview is going well so far. "Um, what exactly would my role there be?" she asks guiltily, like maybe she should know the answer.

If it was a dumb question, he doesn't let on. "Kind of a jack of all trades job, actually," he says. "Everything from retail clerk. Selling gifts, wine of course, T-shirts, that kind of thing. Everything from that to doing what I do – meeting with other buyers, learning about the other wineries, tasting the wine so you know what you're talking about. Heck..." He places the last bottle on the last table, then closes up the box and stuffs it under a table. "I've even been in the field, picking the grapes."

Faith is surprised by that. "I might need to buy some garden gloves," she jokes.

"It wouldn't hurt."

That was as much of an interview as she was going to get. The rest of the time, Faith opened bottles and made conversation with the invitees. She shared what knowledge she could about the different grape varietals when asked. When necessary, she carried dirty glasses down the stairs to a tiny kitchen meant more for one employee to plug in a coffee maker than for a wine drinking crowd like the one mingling about today.

As the crowd thinned, she helped Morty pack up the dirty wine glasses to be delivered to a caterer he rented them from. Then he loaded what was left of the wine into his small car with a surprising amount of back seat space, while she was encouraged to sample some of the wine left in opened bottles.

"Mind my asking where else you are interviewing?" he asks her over a plummy glass of $50 Merlot. They take turns spitting into an urn between them. For this bottle, Faith would have loved to actually swallow, with a fat plate of steak and frites by her side. But it's the middle of the day, and she has a long day still ahead. And alas, no steak and frites.

"Not at all," she says, trying to come up with an answer fast that makes her seem more desirable than she actually is. "This week, The Wine Social Club. In Toronto," she lies, trying to seem nonchalant about it. His reaction is something more akin to amusement than concern, so she may have overplayed the nonchalant card. "And I'm still setting up interviews for next week." She lies again. But it's kind of true, given the feelers she has out. She may get up to 5-6 interviews if every application she made yields something.

"Well, good luck to you," he says, with a clink of his glass on hers.

And that was it. They part with a handshake, exchange full contact information, and he says she'll hear something in the next two weeks.

After he drives off, Faith checks her phone. She has an email from the Wine Club. She smiles as she reads the interview details. So technically, I only lied once to Morty, she thinks.

18
BRIAN

9. If you could change anything about how you were raised, what would it be?

Not a thing. My parents gave me a solid foundation. Mom encouraged my artistic side. Dad gave me the reality check conversations about making a living. We were surrounded by friends and family at the cottage in the summers. In the winters, I worked on academics. And if I struggled with any one, Mom found me tutors. It was a very balanced upbringing. If I am forced to come up with a flaw, and this is just a picky thing. But gun to my head, what would I change? Maybe I should have been shown how to fail a little bit more. You know, allowed to be crazy and careless; make a few mistakes. Other kids, I noticed had less than model parents, and often floundered a bit in life before finding their stride. I pitied them at first. But I don't know. Maybe that's how you learn to feel safe in an unsafe world.|

When Brian gets home, he calls Tanica's name, but there's no answer. He checks the upstairs, office, even the storage area in the basement and the garage. No sign of her. That's weird, he thinks. Maybe she has errands. He sends her a text, "When are you home?"

While he waits for a response, he figures he should deal with the chipmunk. He steps out on to the back patio, the bitter wind snatching at his hair and penetrating his sweater in one breathless gust. He folds his arms around himself and peers into the cage at the bottom edge of the deck. He hears a little rattling and assumes it's the wind. With one arm he covers his mouth and nose, with the other he grabs the metal handle quickly, regretting his lack of gloves, and walks as fast as he can inside, through the back doors and to the garage. More rattling as he walks. Against his better judgment, he looks inside as he nears the compost bin. He can't believe it. The little guy is still alive. Curling up in a corner one second, racing to the other side of the cage the next second.

"Is that how you stayed warm?" he asks the chipmunk, forgetting about covering his nose and mouth. "Alternating between curling up and spazzing out?"

The chipmunk pauses, listening to the sound of his voice, assessing this new potential threat. His little pink nose wiggles as he smells out this new environment. His ears seem to straighten and turn like a rabbit's would. His beady black eyes rest on Brian's for a fraction of a second. Then it crawls tentatively to a corner, curling itself up into a fetal position. All Brian can see of the chipmunk now is the curved arch of its back. It has hidden its head, paws and tail underneath himself. Brian watches its sides for a few seconds to see if it waited until this moment to die. But the chipmunk is breathing, the fluffed-out sides of him pulsing in a rhythmic pattern.

"All right then," Brian says. "Catch and release it is."

He considers the weather and wonders how long the creature can survive if he drops it off in an unfamiliar place. He grabs some newspaper from the recycling bin, shreds it and stuffs some through the tiny holes in the cage, careful not to open the latch. He knows chipmunks can run out in a flash. Then he gets a step ladder and reaches up to the shelf where he keeps the summer bird feeder supplies. He scoops out some sunflower seeds from the giant bag he bought from Walmart in the spring. He pushes the seeds through the little holes one by one. The chipmunk stays curled up, breathing, finally able to sleep.

"That ought to hold you until I think up a solution," Brian says. He sets the cage gently on a lower shelf near the recycling bins. Faith would be proud, he thinks. And then chides himself for forgetting to forget about her.

Back upstairs, he checks his phone. No answer from Tanica yet. It's only 5 o'clock. If she had errands, she'll be home by 6 o'clock, he reasons.

He brings his laptop to the chair by the window. Darkness conceals his view of the river. But knowing it's out there, the wind whipping about in the inkiness between them, gives him peace of mind. He opens an email and types:

To Whom it May Concern:

In accordance with the policies specified in your contract agreement for using the SoulMate app services, I am invoking my right to a full refund.

The lady with whom I was matched is the polar opposite of my type. I wonder if anyone in your company bothers to read the questionnaires that take so much time to complete. Had you read mine, or had a computer digest the data, you would have known without a doubt I cannot be matched with someone who hates Pinot Noir.

Ignoring this glitch, Faith (the supposed soulmate match) is young and immature. She is fussy about food. She is obsessed with animals, while I am allergic to all of them – as you would know if you assimilated the data properly. And she loathes the sophisticated and perfectly balanced Pinot grape that, let's be fair, most respectable wine connoisseurs beyond me appreciate.

To a man who drinks wine casually, an amateur if you will, Faith's flagrant ignorance on the nuances of the Pinot grape might be forgivable. But I am not an amateur and she is trained as a sommelier!

Given that a soulmate match was guaranteed by your company and given that no such match occurred after payment, I demand the return of the entire amount remitted.

Regards,

Brian Lovelace

Brian reads over the email draft before sending. It is a bit harsh, but he cannot afford to leave room for doubt on his position. Sid will be looking for the return of the fee into the Paper's account. And he can't write the article he promised if there's any doubt on the failure of the match.

He hits send and checks his phone for Tanica's text. No reply yet, but he has one from his mother. "Don't forget martini night," it says. "7:00 OK?"

"Sounds good," Brian texts back. "Not sure if Tanica can make it. See you soon."

✳✳✳

Brian clinks his martini glass with Maggie's. "Cheers!" they say together, careful to make the requisite eye contact while doing so, then sip. He has to hand it to his mother. She knows how to make martinis. Slender ice crystals float atop an almost syrupy fusion of Bombay and Vermouth in his glass. This is their second martini. The movie, *Pretty Woman,* for the umpteenth time, (he can't deny his mother the nostalgic comfort of a love story well executed) is on pause. Richard Gere has paid Julia Roberts and sent her packing. (Brian and Maggie had sniffled, almost imperceptibly as always, when Julia said "It was a really good offer" before rejecting him.) The part his mom likes the best is coming up next. ("What does the knight do after he rescues the princess?" Gere will ask. "She rescues him right back," Julia will say.) Brian knows the lines by heart, yet he can't deny their emotional punch, still, after all these years.

"Let me ask you something, Mom," Brian says. "You guys always said I couldn't have pets because I'm allergic, right?"

"Right," she says, setting her glass down on the coffee table, and dipping a shrimp into some cocktail sauce.

"Am I allergic to *all* animals?" he asks. "I mean, surely not turtles, fish–"

"Surely not," she says, taking a small bite of the shrimp, holding a cocktail napkin that has "Wine Wednesday" written on it.

"Is there a list somewhere of my allergies?"

She places her napkin, with the inedible shrimp tail, on the table. "What's this about, Brian? Is that Tanica trying to talk you into a pet?"

"No, nothing like that," Brian says. He thinks about the text he finally received from Tanica before he headed over to Maggie's.

"Sleeping at my place tonight. Had some things to deal with over here," it said. It made perfect sense to Brian. But the vagueness niggles at him. What *things*?

"I caught a chipmunk in the trap is all." He takes another sip. "It's a wonder it survived the cold," he adds, swirling some shrimp in the sauce. "I brought it to the garage and spent some time making sure it was alive and comfortable while I figure out what to do with it." He takes a bite, tosses the tail on the table and chews. "But no hives so far. And my sinuses are clear."

"Except for when Vivian rejected Edward's offer," his mother says, shooting him a playful smile.

Brian can't help but laugh. "You noticed? I tried really hard to hide it this time!"

Maggie's expression changes to concern. She eyes him searchingly over the rim of her glass. "You're wondering if you can keep it as a pet, this chipmunk?" she asks, suspiciously.

"Of course not," he says. "It's just it got me thinking. I've avoided animals my whole life. Maybe I don't have to be so careful around some of them. It would be nice to know which ones I react to, and which ones I don't."

She nods, understanding. "I have a list somewhere, I think. They did a back scratch test, if I recall correctly. I bet they have better methods nowadays. I'll look through my files and let you know what I find."

"Great, thanks Mom."

She picks up the remote and starts to press play. "You never said why Tanica couldn't make it," she casually mentions. Her finger hovers over the play button, her eyes stay on the TV.

"Oh sorry, she was really bummed she couldn't come," he lies. "She had some things to do back at her place."

19
FAITH

10. What's your life story in four minutes or less?

Born to mother, Hope Cooper, and father, Joe Schultz; a result of one drunken Canada Day party. Mom opted to keep me, Joe opted to bolt. I only met him when he showed up for Mom's funeral to see if there was any money left for him. Good riddance. Mom raised me alone, with babysitting help from Bitta (my grandmother) until I was old enough for school, working as an elementary school teacher at the neighbourhood Catholic school until she was too sick to continue. I moved in with Bitta, who counselled me to take school seriously and figure out what I want to do with my life sooner rather than later "because she's not getting any younger." I considered teaching but didn't think I could be around kids all day, so I chose wine where I could work with adults. Not that I hate kids, mind you. I just never had siblings or nieces or nephews, so no real exposure or interest in childhood education. It was hard enough focusing on my own education, lol. Bitta agreed to pay for two years of any post high school program that would "qualify me to get a job and move out." Not that she doesn't love me. I know she does. She just wants to move on with her life. And believes that's the best thing for me too. So I got a degree in business and wine at Algonquin. "Wine won't get you far," Bitta said, and the College had a one-year program for basic business. Now I'm at Farm Boy where I secretly manage wine tasks for free when I have time, and applying to every respectable wine-related job I can find before Bitta kicks me out in two weeks. (Three if I complete this stupid app and make a solid effort to find a love connection, preferably one who isn't dirt poor.) My time is up, but I have to add that although she may joke about it, I know Bitta isn't trying to turn me into a gold-digger. She raised me better than that. Bitta just knows from experience "it's as easy to fall in love with a man with money than a man without," as she so brazenly puts it. Lol.

Seventeen more days until I'm kicked out, Faith notes, as she crosses out another calendar day. She feeds Jasper and checks her to-do's.

Figure out the cheapest way to get to Toronto is first on the list. Although the fancy wine club extended an interview, there was no offer to compensate her travel expenses. Interview is tomorrow, so she needs to lock down transportation and once again switch shifts with someone at Farm Boy. This will be a day killer, but hopefully worth her time. "Club Steward" has a respectable ring to it. *Ka-ching*, she thinks, imagining a salary package with benefits.

The only other to-do is apply for two more jobs. She can do that after work. Faith's proficiency at the job application process had significantly increased with each inquiry. She checks the job openings list she made with Allie. "LCBO Clerk," and "Wine Educator" are up next.

Working at an Ontario Liquor Board store would be great. Government jobs typically have salaries and benefits, she knows. And she could gain experience advising customers on wine, although she would likely be chained to the cash register most of the time. At least she is qualified for this one.

"Wine Educator" is a stretch. She will have to exaggerate her experience to come close to meeting the prerequisites. And she is not interested in teaching at all, she admits. She conjures up a classroom full of wine noobs in her mind, staring her down at the podium in a windowless room, a Power Point page displayed on the screen behind her with the basic palate options. The students' eyes, eager to learn at first, glaze over as they come to understand the tedious regional information they will have to memorize, the long list of varietals and their descriptions, and the step-by-step process that stretches from the harvest to grape juice conversion, that stand between them and the actual tasting part of the course. She shudders. Nightmare, she thinks.

Bitta pokes her head in the door, tentatively. "Oh," she says, "You're already up and showered."

Faith smiles proudly. "And hair styled." She has come so far in the last few days. Less rushing about. Her basic self-care schedule folding neatly now into her routine.

"Have you heard from that soulmate fellow?" Bitta asks sheepishly. Bitta knows the answer. If Faith had heard anything, Bitta would be the first to know.

Faith shakes her head. "I'm working on my transportation for the Toronto interview. Any tips?"

Bitta itches her cheek and eases the door open a little further now that they are on a safe topic. "Flying's out. You can't afford that. The train will cost you a pretty penny, too, but it's cheaper than flying. Sometimes there are student rates."

"I'll take a look," Faith says, making a note on her phone and seeing she has an email alert.

"I'd check buses too," Bitta adds. "Can't be too much to bus, but scrutinize the times. They probably make a lot of stops."

"Good point," Faith says. She pretends to make a note. She can't resist clicking the email to see who it's from.

"Don't go using one of those unsanctioned ride share offers out there on Kijiji or whatever," Bitta says, her voice taking on a stern edge. "God knows what could happen to a pretty young lady in one of those cars. And they are not insured."

"Got it," Faith says. The email is from SpringSide. She doesn't want to alert Bitta she's heard from them already. The interview was only yesterday. It's probably a rejection. "Anything else?"

"You must be busy," Bitta says, gesturing to the giant calendar over Faith's bed, with the countdown exes and to-do's. "I should leave you to it."

"Thanks, Bitta," Faith says. "I do need to finalize this travel issue before work if possible."

"Of course." Bitta starts to leave, hesitates, then re-opens the door a smidge. "Would you mind coming with me to Euchre night over at the church?" she asks. "Matthew hates churches, you know how he is."

Faith doesn't know, but okay, she thinks, let Bitta finish so I can look at the email.

"And you're pretty good at it."

"Thanks to a good teacher," Faith adds, flattering Bitta.

"Anyway, it's day after tomorrow. At seven or so. It would mean a lot to me if you could be my partner." She looks up at the calendar, where Faith's work schedule is posted, confirming her availability. "If nothing more important comes up," she adds without appearing to mean it.

Faith enjoys this softer side of Bitta. She doesn't see it often. They both know Bitta could have said, "I need you at the Euchre game. If you have plans, change them," and Faith would comply.

"There's no place I'd rather be," Faith says, putting down her phone and hopping on to her bed. "Euchre with Bitta, 7:00," she writes, and goes to give Bitta a hug.

Bitta waves her away. "Don't go all mushy on me. It's only Euchre," Bitta says. Just before she closes the door, Faith swears she sees Bitta wink.

She clicks on the email, steeling herself for bad news. It is not bad news. Well, not all bad. The email contains a formal job offer, full time! But, and here's the bad news, almost apologetically the email references the minimum wage salary that accompanies the position, suggesting intangible benefits that the winery owner hopes will be of interest to Faith. She wonders if she could find a place to live in Niagara on that compensation. She would certainly need a roommate. She will have to look at housing options later. For now, she needs to keep this offer (A legitimate offer! At an actual winery!) in her back pocket while she investigates the Toronto option.

She decides she should reply right away. They may be disorganized enough to extend the offer to someone else before she has a chance to accept if she waits too long.

"Thank you for your generous offer," Faith types. She imagines it is generous to them, remembering Morty's jack-of-all-trades description of the staffing roles there. Employees with expanded job descriptions denotes limited budgets. "I am very interested. Before committing, I will need some time to investigate the apartment rental market in your area." She looks up at her calendar. Two-and-a-half weeks before she's homeless. "Can I get back to you in a week?" She knows it's unprofessional, how she is handling this, but she doesn't have the luxury of time to consult with Allie on job search correspondence protocols.

She presses send and checks the time. Her shift starts in an hour. She should leave now to give herself time to bus, (she can check transportation options as she rides) find someone to take tomorrow's shift, and see what interesting wines showed up in the stockroom overnight.

As she reaches for her puffy coat, her phone rings. It's an unidentified number. She gets those from time to time, but it could be important. Maybe from the Toronto people. She considers letting it roll to Voicemail. She is anxious to get to work and doesn't want to listen politely to some random telemarketer long enough to say she's not interested. She's one or two steps away from being that poor sap, making call after call to rude people in hopes of a sale, taking abuse to make ends meet. Hanging up or ignoring their calls is not an option for her. But it could be the Toronto people offering to arrange transportation, which would save her a load of time. Unlikely but still.

"Hello," she says, grabbing her coat and sliding her feet into her Uggs.

"May I speak with Faith Cooper?"

She rolls her eyes, ready for the sales pitch onslaught. "Speaking."

"Sorry to bother you, Miss Cooper. I'm calling on behalf of SoulMate regarding your match arrangements."

"Yes?" Faith says. She is confused. Why would the app people call her? Some sort of survey, perhaps?

"Brian has asked for a refund. He claims the match was a failure. I'm calling to verify your agreement that the match failed. From your perspective, of course."

Before Faith can think twice, she blurts out, "No, it wasn't a failure. He's just a jerk."

"I see," says the voice, detached and robotic, unsympathetic.

"There was a definite connection," she explains, surprised at how hard her heart is beating, how much red her eyes are seeing, at how an obvious connection could so quickly unravel with one unceremonious rejection. She forces herself to breathe and think logically. This isn't about her. It's about him. "Do you mind telling me why he thinks it was a failure?" She knows he felt it too. Maybe not by the end of the date. But definitely at the beginning.

"Says here," the voice says (Faith imagines a screen being pulled up with all her data, all of *his* data.), "that Mr. Lovelace..."

There is a pause while the voice, obviously a man, gives a small snort of amusement. "...and yourself disagree on the critical issue of Pinot Noir."

Something about this makes Faith laugh, despite the outrageousness of Brian's excuse, *because* of the outrageousness of his excuse. She is out the door and halfway to the bus stop by the time her original panic from this rejection subsides. Her hands are freezing. She can't hold the phone and put her mitts on at the same time. Better make this quick. "If Mr. Lovelace is so convinced I'm all wrong for him over the issue of Pinot Noir," Faith says, "please give him my best and ask him to do me the small courtesy of refraining from the killing of chipmunks in the future."

"Chipmunks?" the voice asks.

"Thanks for your call," Faith says, and hangs up.

20
BRIAN

10. What's your life story in four minutes or less?

I can tell it in two. Born and raised in Ottawa by supportive parents. Attended Ryerson University for Journalism. Hired by Ottawa's top newspaper upon graduation, where I remain to this day as Political Reporter. My father died two years ago, as previously mentioned, mother alive and well. I have good friends, a good job, own my house, and enjoy reasonable success as a writer. I am ready to settle down, get married and start a family. Less than 30 seconds, actually.|

Brian wakes up with a start in the morning, realizing the chipmunk has no water. Dehydration kills a creature faster than hunger, he knows. How could he be so stupid? He gets up and puts on his housecoat quickly, registering a stab of pain at Tanica's still made side of the bed, and rushes downstairs.

He doesn't have a water bottle meant for an animal cage. And he can't open the cage without risking the creature's escape anyhow. He paces around the kitchen, opening cabinets and studying the water faucet, arriving at no conclusion that would work. He stares out the window above the kitchen helplessly and notices the snow.

Bolting down the stairs and out the front door, he scoops up a handful of snow and hurries back inside, cursing himself for not bringing a cup or something to put the snow in. In the garage, he checks to see if the chipmunk is breathing. It is, thank God. (Why does he care so much?)

The chipmunk is awake, hovering in a corner with a nest of newspaper scraps arranged around him. Brian's hands are burning with cold. He shoves the snow through the holes at the opposite end from the nest. Some of it melts onto the floor of the cage immediately but not much. The rest clings to the outside of the cage and Brian's fingers. He wipes his hand on the terry cloth fabric of his housecoat and waits to see if the chipmunk moves.

It stares at him with suspicious beady eyes. Brian shoves his numb hands into his pockets. He is about to head back indoors and look for another solution, when the chipmunk darts out of its nest and inspects the tiny puddle on the other side. He dips into the puddle greedily.

Brian exhales, only now realizing he's been holding his breath. The snow on the outside of the cage is melting already, but the majority drops to the garage floor. It's not a permanent solution, he thinks. But hopefully it bought him some time.

Back upstairs he checks his phone. His interview with the SoulMate ex-employee is at 10 o'clock. That gives him a couple of hours to figure out this chipmunk fiasco and check in with Tanica. Checking his inbox to make sure the guy hasn't chickened out and canceled the interview, he's surprised to find a reply from SoulMate to his refund request so soon.

Dear Mr. Lovelace,

We have received your refund request and contacted Miss Cooper to verify the match failure. Miss Cooper does not agree that the match failed.

As you know from the terms of the agreement, our refunds are permitted in the event both parties, not one, are dissatisfied. As Miss Cooper expressed no such dissatisfaction, the refund option is not available. It is customary to allow both parties a chance to reflect on the date before concluding the match is devoid of soulmate potential.

Nevertheless, given the clarity of your position on Miss Cooper's objectionable qualities, we are willing to make an exception and grant your refund request. The money will appear in the account from which it was remitted within two business days. Please note, under the terms of the agreement, you are forbidden any voluntary and/or planned contact with Miss Cooper from this day forward. Should voluntary and/or planned contact be uncovered by our top notch investigative team, full payment of the original fees plus a $500 penalty will become immediately due and payable by you. I'm sure you can understand SoulMate retains all rights to collect said amount, via the judicial process if necessary, in the event it is not remitted in a timely manner.

Should you decide, upon further reflection, that the soulmate potential between you and Miss Cooper does exist before receipt of your refund, you must notify SoulMate in a timely manner to avoid further penalties arising from voluntary and/or planned contact with Miss Cooper.

Thank you in advance for your compliance with the provisions in our app agreement. And of course, please accept our sincere apologies for any inconvenience incurred during the SoulMate process.

With Kind Regards,

The SoulMate Evaluation Team

P.S. A member of our resolution team wishes to convey Miss Cooper's message, upon receiving notice of your rejection, to "please give him my best and ask him to do me the small courtesy of refraining from the killing of chipmunks in the future."

But it is not dead, ha! Brian thinks. *Yet.* Her message stirs up amusement and anger in him. He can't decide whether to laugh or curse. There is no time for either, anyway, if he's going to get to the interview on time. Mentally, he checks off return-of-refund on his list and heads for the shower.

Once dressed and ready for the interview, Brian phones Tanica. She picks up on the first ring. "Hi," she says. "I'm just now walking into the salon. Everything okay?"

"All good," Brian says, *oblivion* popping into his head as he speaks. I'm *aware* we have things to discuss, Brian tells himself. Now is not the time. "Did you get things sorted out at home?"

"Yes, yes, thanks for asking," Tanica says, the drone of hair dryers rising up in the background. Brian notices she doesn't elaborate on what *things*.

"Okay then. Just wanted to check in. Missed you last night. Mom invited us for one of her martini nights." He manages an insincere laugh. "We watched her favourite movie again. She was disappointed you couldn't be there. I gave her your regrets."

Tanica speaks to the receptionist at the salon, asking about messages and cancellations. "That's nice," she says to Brian. "I really have to go, darling."

"Of course," Brian says. "Oh, one more thing," he says.

"What, Brian," her voice laced with impatience.

"It's too cold to release the chipmunk we caught. I'm trying to keep it alive until I figure out what to do with it. Any ideas? I'm a little stumped, and there's no way to give it water without opening the cage and risking its escape."

There's a long pause. Long enough for Brian to feel guilty for bothering her with such a silly issue. "Take it to a wildlife place?" she suggests. "Humane society or something?"

Brian brightens at the obvious solution. She is a smart one, his girlfriend. "Yes, great idea! I'll make some calls. Thanks, my love."

"All right," she says. "Bye now," and hangs up.

Brian grabs his coat and gets in his car, checking once more that the chipmunk is breathing. As the garage door goes up, he sees his mother in the review mirror walking on the side walk. She waves at him as she passes. He notices she is taking tentative steps on the icy sidewalk. He opens his door and yells, "Where are you headed, Mom?"

She peers out of the hooded Canada Goose coat he gave her for Christmas. "Meeting at church."

"Do you have to go, Mom?" he says. "It's really cold. And icy."

She waves this comment off with her fleecy pink mitt. "What am I going to do? Sit inside all winter because of weather?"

"At least let me drive you," Brian says.

She stands aside while he reverses the car out of the garage and unlocks the passenger door for her to get in. "You really needn't bother," she says, placing her bottom on the seat first and sliding her legs in after. "I know how to handle weather."

He drives her to church, drilling her about her schedule for the next couple of days. He doesn't like to think of her falling on the ice. Breaking a hip is too common in women her age, and he knows a good number of those women die from their injuries.

"I'm signed up to bring snacks to Euchre night," she says. "I don't want to miss that."

Brian pictures her navigating the sidewalk with a Tupperware of muffins. "Let me drive you to that," he says.

"No way," she objects. "You have a life."

"Just so happens I'm free that night," he says. "I don't want to brag, but I play a mean Euchre game."

To his relief, she does laugh instead of putting up a bigger fight. "That would be fun," she says. "Thank you." They arrive at the church, Brian sees the sidewalks are properly salted, so he lets her open the door herself and feel her way out of the car. "My friends are going to have a field day when they see you," she says before closing the door. "Not one of them has a more handsome or thoughtful son."

21
FAITH

11. If you could wake up tomorrow having gained any one quality or ability, what would it be?

That's easy. Hair that doesn't turn into a giant frizz ball without a half hour of blow-drying.|

On the way to work, Faith determines the round trip cost for her interview in Toronto is affordable if she takes advantage of the special deals she sees online. But Bitta was right. The train is more reliable. If she can get Allie or Bitta to drive her to the station, and pick her up, she can leave Ottawa tomorrow morning and get to her interview with plenty of time to get lost, get stalled on the tracks by random cows or whatever the winter equivalent of that would be, and navigate the Toronto mass transit to her destination. She texts Allie, secures her availability, and buys the tickets online. That's one item off her list. Next up, getting out of tomorrow's shift.

"Hi Chad," she says on her way to the time clock. Between Bitta's interruption this morning, the email reply to SpringSide, the aggravating SoulMate call, and the sluggish adherence to any prescribed schedule that accompanies Ottawa mass transit in general and after a snowfall in particular, the universe conspired to get her to work too late for stealing Chad's wine stocking job.

Chad looks up from an open box of ugli fruit. "What gives?" he says. "I had to stock all the stupid wine *and* give up my smoke break."

"I take issue with the word *break*," Faith says. "And I'm sorry. A bunch of things came up this morning I hadn't counted on. Is Angela here?"

"No," he says. "We are understaffed, apparently. You may be the only cashier until Monique makes it in. She had *issues* with childcare," he says, rolling his eyes.

"Ugh," Faith says, stamping her time card and grabbing her register envelope from the open office next to it, "I need coverage for tomorrow. I have an interview in Toronto."

Chad inspects a box marked brussels sprouts, makes a grossed out face, and closes the box fast. "Dammit. These things reek!"

Faith heads for the doors, "Someone is a grouchy grouch when he doesn't get his smoke *break*," she says, using air quotes.

Before she makes it through the doors, Chad says, "Wait," and walks over to her. "Let me help you with that."

Faith eyes him suspiciously. "An envelope? You're helping me carry an envelope?"

"Just walk with me then."

Together, they walk through the doors. "Okay, what's going on?" Faith says. She has a nose for weirdness. And this is weird.

"Nothing. I just want to say sorry for snapping at you," Chad says. "You don't deserve it"

"Okay? Apology accepted?"

As they walk through the cereal aisle, which towers above the others, concealing them from the eyes of Stella and any others going about their duties in the store, Chad stops her with his hand on her shoulder. "I'm also wondering if you are free sometime? For a movie or something."

Faith doesn't know what to say. Is Chad even old enough to drink? She doesn't want to ask. That would be mean. He is cute though. She takes in for the first time his curly dark hair, his whisper of a moustache, and his not terrible muscular physique.

When was the last time she had a date, anyway? Forgetting for a moment Brian. She can't remember. Did she date anyone since she graduated? She could use the practice. Obviously, she is rusty at it, considering the stellar rejection she received this morning.

"Sure," she says. "Let's do that."

Leaving one happy young man in the cracker aisle (He's at least 16, right? She'll have to ask Stella and maybe look up the statutory rape laws.), Faith sets up her cash register and notes no other cashier doing the same. Panic starts to set in that she won't find a shift replacement. What if she calls in sick? What if they find out? What if she gets fired? No need to panic, she tells herself. Hopefully, Monique is available. And Chad owes her one. She could convince him to let her train him if nothing else pans out by the end of the day. All sorts of options, she thinks with a smile.

A real live male person does not find her repulsive. She needed that today.

22
BRIAN

11. If you could wake up tomorrow having gained any one quality or ability, what would it be?

I can't think of a quality or ability that I would care to magically wake up with. If there were a quality or ability I aspire to attain, I would figure out how to achieve it and put in the hard work. Even as a kid, I wasn't interested in superheroes with obscurely obtained powers. Batman was the only superhero I followed with any interest. And Bruce Wayne spent years training to perfect his moves. He used his brain developing the weapons and vehicles he used to get around. And he used his social skills to form connections that enabled him to complete his heroic missions. So I guess it's not in me to dream up magically acquired abilities. I'd prefer to work within the realms of reality.|

"You're kidding me," Brian says. After depositing his mother safely in front of the church doors, he dialed up the Ottawa Humane Society on Bluetooth. "You don't deal with wild animals? What if I told you it's a tame animal. A chipmunk that begs for treats, for example." He suddenly remembers an Instagram page Vivia once showed him – a pet squirrel. It had a leash and cuddled with its owner. "Walks on a leash?"

"I'm sorry," the volunteer phone answerer says. "We don't take in chipmunks."

He imagines she has a list of acceptable animals on a sheet she cannot deviate from. "So you'd rather let a chipmunk die from dehydration or exposure than accept it?" he asks, playing the guilt card.

"Wild creatures live in the wild for a reason. They adapt," she says, flatly, like she's been to the guilt-card rodeo before.

Brian pulls into the parking lot of Tim Hortons, the location his source specified for meeting. It's the quietest looking, most suburban Tim Hortons he's ever seen. No danger of being overheard by SoulMate corporate types here, he thinks. "Okay, I get it," he tells the OHS volunteer. "If you don't take in wild animals, who does?"

"You could try the Wild Animal Refuge?" she says.

"Great," he says. He could have googled for a more helpful nugget than that obvious gem. "Thank you for your time." He disconnects the call.

He pulls up his notes for the meeting on his phone. He doesn't want to spook this guy by looking too organized. He wants to create a comfortable atmosphere with lots of chitchat, talk about the weather and how the Sens are doing this year (every Ottawa male he knows will talk hockey to anyone anytime) before bringing up his questions.

Inside the doors, he sees only one customer in the dining area – a middle-aged gentleman with hipster glasses, a coffee cup in front of him. Brian waves and the man waves back. Guess that's my guy, he thinks. To set the man at ease, he orders a black coffee and a box of Timbits. The most basic order a customer could make at Tim's. Should look pretty normal to the average customer who shows up.

"Mr. Weiss?" he asks. The man nods, and Brian offers him a Timbit.

He selects a sour cream one and says thank you, placing the glazed donut hole on the napkin Brian hands him. Brian takes the seat across from him.

"I appreciate your taking the time to talk to me, Mr. Weiss."

"Please, call me Don."

"Thank you. I'm Brian. Nice to meet you, Don," he says. They shake hands.

Before Brian can comment on the cold snap Ottawa is having, Don says, "Let's get to the point. I don't have long." He smiles curtly and folds his hands together in front of him on the table.

"All right," Brian says. Here we go, he thinks. "As I mentioned on the phone, I am doing a story on the app. It's quite popular, yet no one knows anything about it."

"The science is patented. It's not a matter of public knowledge how it works," Don says. "I can't help with those sorts of questions without violating my confidentiality agreement with the company."

"Yes, I suspected that. It's just that it's unusual that I can't find any record of the persons behind the company. Plenty of shell type corporations, but no actual names of people."

"That is by design," Don says. "Shell corporations discourage frivolous lawsuits and protect the principals from personal liability."

Brian nods. "Of course you're right." He takes a sip of his coffee. "It would be nice to have a quote from the company for my article. Do you have any names you could give me? Someone with authority who can comment?"

"No," Don says. "Also covered by the confidentiality provisions."

"I see," Brian says, scratching his head. He figured this would be a dead end. "Well, I won't trouble you any further then. Sorry to drag you out in this weather for such a short meeting."

"Do you mind my asking what the article is about?" Don says, as Brian stands to leave.

Brian sits down and contemplates the question. It's a risk being honest with this guy, but it may be the only way he gets anything useful out of him. He decides to level with him. "We have evidence the app doesn't *actually* connect soulmates, that any successes relate to perhaps tricks of psychology, if you will, brainwashing people desperate to fall in love into thinking they are in love when they get a date, regardless of any science associated with selecting the supposed match." Brian pauses to give Don a chance to respond to this. "We were hoping to get a quote from an actual representative of the company before going forward with the story."

Don looks down at his hands folded on the table. Brian hears donuts hitting a vat of hot grease, an abrupt sizzling sound that slowly fades away. He doesn't take his eyes off Don for fear of missing something.

"Interesting," Don finally says. "I wonder...is psychology not a science?"

23
FAITH

12. If a crystal ball could tell the truth about yourself, your life, the future or anything else, what would you want to know?

Will I get the opportunity to work in a proper wine career job and if so, will that happen before I'm out on the street, where securing a job will be immensely more difficult? And if it's not too much trouble, crystal ball, do I have a soulmate, and if so where can I find him? That's two questions. I feel like I should get two here, considering I'll know eventually, if I ever finish this questionnaire, if the soulmate thing works out. But assuming the career/homelessness issue gets resolved, I'd really like an answer to the second question. Lol.|

Toronto's Wine Social Club looks nothing like Faith imagined. She double-checks the address on her phone and scrutinizes the address on the house she stands in front of once again.

It doesn't look like a business, let alone club. No parking lot, no fancy pillars, no lettering outside the plain front doors to identify it as anything other than a residence.

She knocks on the door and waits, noticing a toddler sized tricycle nestled in the bushes off the front steps. The door flies open and a frazzled looking woman with a baby on her hip stands before her. "Yes?" the lady says.

"Hi," Faith says, flustered. "I may be at the wrong place here. I have a meeting with Penelope of the Wine Social Club at…" (She checks her phone. Crap, she's going to be late.)

"That's me," Penelope says, "Come in."

Faith stays where she is. "Are you sure?"

The baby fusses, and Penelope switches it to the other hip. "Am I sure I'm Penelope?"

"That this is the Wine Social Club," Faith says.

"Yes, yes, come in, please," Penelope says, gesturing for Faith to follow.

Faith steps inside and shuts the door behind her. There's a trail of toys between the front door and the place at the end of a hallway Penelope disappeared into. She picks her way around the toys and down the hall.

"Is that your usual pace?" Penelope asks, pulling a bottle out of a pan on the stove and holding it against the baby's lips. "You need to keep up."

Before Faith can respond, Penelope takes off again through another door from the kitchen and leads her through a dining room, past a bathroom and up the stairs, talking faster than Faith can take in the entire way. "That's the dining room. Where the guests will be. That's the powder room. You've seen the kitchen. You'll find the dish soap under the sink. Did I say where the wine glasses are? They're in the dining room hutch. And up here are the bedrooms. If anyone gets too drunk, they can sleep in the guest room."

She takes off back down the stairs again, leaving Faith no choice but to follow. She stays close to Penelope's heels, waiting for a gap in the non-stop directions to ask what in the name of God she is talking about. "Down here," Penelope continues, leading Faith down the basement stairs past the powder room, "is the wine cellar…" She gestures to a corner of the dank storage area where several LCBO bags, rest on a card table. "You'll serve the white first, followed by the red. Take a look and make sure you know the varietals and the history…"

"Hold up!" Faith shouts, stopping Penelope in her tracks and prompting the baby on her hip to drop its bottle and cry. "I'm sorry to interrupt, but I can't quite discern what is happening here. I'm meant to have an interview about a wine steward position at a Club. This…" She waves her arm around helplessly toward the boxes and yard equipment and (what?) rat traps strewn around her. "…does not look like a club, and this doesn't feel like an interview."

"Interview?" Penelope shouts over the child's wailing. "No, this IS a residence. My wine club members show up in just a few hours. I thought it was understood you'd be serving the guests and running the tasting. We have a meeting every month."

Faith's mouth is open. Incredulous. "You're hiring me for a meeting that happens once a month?" she asks. "In your house?"

Penelope looks at Faith likes she's a complete idiot. "Yes, what did you think?"

***

Back on the train, heading back to Ottawa, Faith texts with Allie, miserable about the misunderstanding.

"That's really weird," Allie texts back. "How did we confuse Wine Club with a meeting of desperate young moms meeting to drink wine?"

"Right?" Faith texts. She decides she needs to shake this off and refocus. Obviously, that was not a real wine job. Even if she were desperate enough to go along, she could never afford to live in Toronto, not even in a terrible neighbourhood with a bajillion roommates, with a job that pays minimum wage one evening a month. "At least I have the SpringSide offer. That can't turn out to be worse than this." When Allie doesn't respond right away, Faith adds, "Can it?"

Finally, Allie replies. "Sorry. Googling the winery. It looks legit. They have at least five employees. It's kind of cute."

"Cute." Faith replies. "I'll take cute over what I just walked out of." Faith's phone rings. She texts quickly, "TTL, I have a call."

"Faith. Where the hell are you?" her Farm Boy boss shouts into the phone.

"I'm at a job interview," Faith says. "Monique's filling in for me?"

"I called Monique," he says. "She says no she is not working for you today."

"Oh God. I'm sorry," Faith says. "She told me she would. Maybe we miscommunicated."

There's no response on the phone and Faith can hear his heavy angry breathing. "You're going to need to come in."

"What? I'm in Toronto," Faith says. "Can't Chad do it? I gave him a little training session yesterday before I talked to Monique, just in case."

"And who would do Chad's job?"

Faith flounders at this question. She can't seem to come up with any scenario that might work here.

"Get in here or find another job," he says and hangs up.

Faith lets the phone fall into her lap and stares out the window. The odd house drifts past. Phone lines come and go. Patches of frozen grey ground slowly meld into a consistent stream of snowscape the closer she gets to Ottawa. Eventually, she looks at her inbox, hoping for some kind of inspiration. There is an email from SpringSide, agreeing to give her a week. But no other emails suggest an opportunity for work, let alone interview. She hits reply on the SpringSide interview and types. "Thank you for the time to assess. I accept your generous offer and look forward to the details." Before she signs off, she adds, "Are you aware of any affordable apartments in your area?" She doesn't have a car, she remembers. "Preferably, within walking distance?"

She starts a text to Allie, tries to decide how to condense what just happened in the fewest possible words, when an email alert pops up. It's from SpringSide. That was fast. "There's an apartment at the winery that's included with the job," it says. "I would have mentioned it, but figured you wanted to find your own place in Niagara. I am pleased you will be working for us, Faith. Morty has nothing but good things to say about you. I'll put an employment package in the mail tomorrow, overnight mail. Let's speak on the phone after you've had a chance to look it over and discuss the particulars. Best Regards, Samuel."

24
BRIAN

12. If a crystal ball could tell the truth about yourself, your life, the future or anything else, what would you want to know?

As there is no such thing as a crystal ball, I cannot say. I am hopeful the present circumstances of my life will continue as they have so far. Any misfortunes that come my way I trust myself to navigate with the coping skills I've developed over time. Any fortuitous surprises I will embrace with cheer. Futures are a mystery by nature, are they not? What would be the point of life if we knew what our futures hold?|

Jensen slides an envelope toward Brian along the bar's smooth wooden surface at the Whalesbone Restaurant on Elgin. He and Vivia had chosen a pub night alternative well. Jensen's seared scallops over sautéed greens complimented his glass of Trentino

Pinot Nero faultlessly. Jensen and Vivia splurged and shared a bottle with him, and tried to convince Brian of its superb compatibility with their order of chicken wings as persuasively as they could.

After Jensen ordered a round of Scotch for the three of them, ("It's on me," he said, when Brian protested) he exchanged an odd look with Vivia that Brian was in too good of a mood to assess, before handing over the envelope.

"What's this?" Brian says as their scotches arrive.

"First," Jensen says, a toast. "To my two best buddies. May our words e'er be honest and our transgressions quickly forgiven!"

Brian shifts in his seat to get a better look at Jensen's face, and Vivia's. They both have a deer-in-the-headlights possibly drank-too-much look about them. "Well, you've given worse toasts," Brian says and holds up his glass. They clink, lock eyes, and take a sip.

As Brian savours the buttery sting, Jensen and Vivia down their glasses in one swallow.

He looks at the envelope before him, a sudden dread creeping across his chest.

"I've got bad news," Jensen says, as Brian takes out the photographs. He knows before he looks at them. It's over with Tanica.

✳✳✳

Brian wanders through his house like a restless ghost. Tanica's personal effects – there were fewer of them than he realized – sit at the end of his driveway in two cardboard boxes.

He looks at them one last time from his doorway before allowing himself to write her off forever. He scoops up some snow and brings it inside for the chipmunk. He is pleased to see there's still a small puddle where the last snow melted. It's not efficient, but the snow will sustain the little guy until Wildlife Refuge comes tomorrow.

The doorbell rings and he opens the garage door. "Hi Mom," he says. "Ready for some Euchre?"

25
FAITH

13. Is there something you've dreamed of doing for a long time? Why haven't you done it?

I've been dreaming of a career in wine since I graduated a year ago. I've applied to a number of jobs and am starting to wonder if I'll be working at Farm Boy the rest of my life. Perhaps even applying for the Wine Buyer job there some day if it becomes available. But that doesn't really smack of "dream," now does it? If Bitta hadn't put a gun to my head with the homeless threat of hers, I may not have asked Allie to help sort my life out, and I may not have completed this questionnaire and created a calendar to-do system that makes my dream of a real job less of a lark. No more excuses for me. I'm going to do this. I kind of have to, but still. Lol.|

"You coming or not?" Bitta yells from the living room. Faith grabs her puffy coat and finds Bitta standing in the front doorway, stomping her foot.

"Okay, okay, don't get your Depends in a bunch," Faith says.

Bitta gives Faith a stern look. "If I didn't know you had a real job heading your way, I'd kick you to the curb right now," she says, and takes off down the steps. Faith laughs and follows along behind her.

The church basement is abuzz with conversation as Euchre partners stalk the wobbly card tables for the weakest looking competitors. Bitta yells, "Hello, Maggie," to a smartly dressed lady in the kitchen taking scones out of a Tupperware and placing them on a platter.

"You ready to lose?" Maggie calls though the pass-through window between the kitchen and card playing area.

"In your dreams," Bitta fires back. "Where are you setting up? Faith and I may as well beat you first."

Maggie laughs and points to a table in the corner where someone, apparently her partner, is already sitting. She comes out of the kitchen with the platter and offers them a scone before setting the platter down on the snack table.

"You didn't poison these, did you?" Bitta asks, as the three of them head to the table, mouths full of flakey blueberry pastry.

"Ha, ha," Maggie says. "Brian, I want you to meet my friend, Elizabeth. She and her granddaughter think they can beat us at Euchre. Should we give them a chance?"

Brian turns away from the cards he's sorting and locks eyes with Faith. His eyes widen and Faith detects a sheen of sweat on his brow. Her breath catches in her throat as she struggles to control the whirl of emotion in her head. Brian recovers first, holding out his hand. "Hi, I'm Brian." He shakes Bitta's hand and then Faith's. "Well, they look like worthy opponents," he says to Maggie. "But we're a hard team to beat."

26
BRIAN

13. Is there something you've dreamed of doing for a long time? Why haven't you done it?

"Brian works for the paper," Maggie says, after Elizabeth unscrews a bottle of red and sets four glasses on the table. Brian is still processing Elizabeth's news about Faith's job.

"This calls for a toast," Maggie said.

"Wine at a church, really?" Faith said.

"If Catholics didn't drink wine, I wouldn't be Catholic," Elizabeth said.

But it's all a blur to Brian. Seeing Faith again has brought back their first encounter in vivid detail. With Tanica out of the picture, he realizes how blind he was to his obvious connection to Faith. But he can't very well undo the damage he has done now, can he?

"Really," Faith says. "Written anything good lately?" He can't read Faith's expression with the cards in front of her face. "I call… clubs," she says, levelling her eyes on Brian's.

Elizabeth harrumphs. "I was rather hoping you'd let me make the call," she says, extracting a card and placing it under the pile from the deck she just dealt from.

"He did a scathing exposé that went bacterial," Maggie says.

"Viral," Brian says, holding his cards higher near his face to hide his shame.

"Oh yes," Faith says. "I read that one. Interesting."

Elizabeth whispers loudly to Maggie, "I made Faith sign up for that app. Didn't go so well. But at least she got one date out of it. She has a date with another fellow tomorrow. Are you single, Brian?"

Brian visibly blushes and says, "Yes, matter of fact I am."

"Just unloaded a cheater of a girlfriend," Maggie volunteers, taking a sip of her wine.

"Really," Faith says. "You had a girlfriend?"

Brian says, "I was oblivious. Her cheating was obvious to everyone but me." He peers over his cards at Faith, "I have a history, I'm afraid, of ignoring obvious signs when it comes to affairs of the heart."

Faith's turn to blush. "Well, I hope she didn't break your heart. I can't imagine a worse feeling than being rejected."

Ouch, Brian thinks.

Suddenly, it's clear to him. How he feels. What he wants. He knows it may blow up in his face, but he is done being oblivious. He is done playing it safe. He puts his cards down on the table and speaks directly to Faith, as if the elderly partners aren't even there. "Miss Cooper," he says. "If I may be so bold. I would very much enjoy being your date tomorrow night. If you are inclined to reschedule, that is, or if I might succeed in winning your heart, cancel with the other fellow."

Maggie's jaw drops open. Elizabeth's does the same. Faith places her cards on the table face down and takes a long drink from her wine glass. She wrinkles her cute little nose and says, "God, this is terrible wine. Is it Pinot Noir?"

The women stare at her with confused expressions. They can't seem to track what's transpiring between their partners.

Brian smiles. "If it is, I'll find you any other grape you like. If you don't like Pinot, then it's obviously not worthy of you."

Faith smiles, as the older women swivel their heads in her direction. "How gallant," she says. "You aren't by chance an axe murderer or rodent killer, are you? I should know what I'm getting into if I say yes."

Heads swivel back to Brian. But before he can answer, Maggie says, "That reminds me. I found that allergy information you asked about, Brian. You're allergic to everything except gerbils. Isn't that funny?"

Brian doesn't laugh, but keeps his eyes fixed on Faith when he replies. "That's a relief. What about chipmunks?"

Maggie says, "They're not on the list, dear. I'm sorry. Are you still nursing that chipmunk you thought you froze?"

"He goes to the rescue tomorrow," Brian replies, eyes still locked with Faith's. "I'm sad to see him go. I was becoming attached to the little fellow."

Any dream I've ever had, I chased after it. Once I know what I'm shooting for, I do my best to make it happen. If I succeed, I know I did well. If I fail, well I haven't experienced a lot of failure in my life, but I suspect I'd seize every chance I'm given to turn that failure into something beautiful. So no, there isn't something I've dreamed of doing for a long time. If there was, I'd be doing it.

EPILOGUE

"David Muir? That was your pick for dinner?" Brian steps away from the train and sets down his backpack. His Lululemon dress pants hug his toned body in all the right places. His shirt sleeves are rolled up. The contrast between his crisp white shirt and tanned forearms stirs a fire in Faith's body. His hands grip his hips in mock outrage as Faith rushes toward him.

She collapses into his arms, and there they stay, locked in a tight embrace. They sway together, their bodies striving for the closest hug possible. He presses his nose into her hair, breathing in her sunshine scent. She squeezes her cheek to his chest, listening to his breath, his heart.

Finally, she pulls away and smiles up at him. "Hey, I picked a cute journalist with a beard for my optimal dinner companion. That's pretty much you." They had been texting throughout his

130

journey from Ottawa to Niagara, confessing their answers to the SoulMate app questions.

He tries to pull her back in for a hug and she resists, placing a palm against his chest. "Donald Trump though. I don't know how you explain that."

Brian smirks and pulls her into a kiss. They savour the moment, their parted lips gently touching, the rightness of their chemistry pulsing through them.

"We're not going to have our first fight now, are we?" Brian says. He picks up his bag, suddenly aware they are the only two left on the landing.

Faith laughs. She grabs his hand, pulling him toward the parking lot. "Let's just put a bookmark on that one," she jokes. "How was your trip?"

"Not bad. Managed to get an article written. Enjoyed a wee bottle of wine. Had a nap. Seven hours, wow. You couldn't have found a closer winery to work at?" Brian spots the SpringSide Winery van. Its bumble-bee logo winks in the sunlight.

Faith unlocks the passenger side. "We've been over this."

"I know." Brian heaves his backpack into the van. "Have to put a bookmark on that one too." He reaches out to pull her into a hug.

She complies at first, then unravels from his intoxicating embrace. "We should get going. I made reservations for 8:30, birthday boy."

He watches her open the driver side and slide in. She shrugs off her denim jacket, revealing a sexy black sheath dress. Its stretchy fabric leaves no curve to his imagination. "Can't we just celebrate in your apartment?" He wants to be close to her again so badly. How much time stands between now and the after-dinner unsheathing he wonders. "You are all I want for my birthday." He snakes a hand across her thigh.

She slaps his hand away, but her freckled flush betrays her desire. "Don't make this so hard. I have to drive!"

"After dinner, I have you all to myself this weekend, right?" He folds his hands together as she starts the van.

"Right." Faith pulls out of the parking lot and onto the highway. "Sam's giving me the time off." Her eyes shine. She vibrates with energy. He can barely take looking at her. "He did say not to ask for a weekend off for awhile. Weekends are peak hours."

Brian looks out at the rolling pastures, trying to picture her little vineyard apartment nestled there. "We'll have to make this weekend count, then."

She aims a sheepish glance his way. "Oh yes, let's make it count. For Sam."

As the pastures morph into vineyards and the roads turn to dirt and gravel, they talk non-stop. He asks about the chipmunk. "Chippy spends more time on my shoulder than the aviary I built for him," she says. "But the slightest move to pet him sends him darting back to his nest."

She asks about Jasper. "Still not allergic," he reports. "And he's warming up to me, I think. He only bit me once yesterday."

"Aw, I miss Jasper. But I think it's sweet we share custody." She frowns. "Hope it doesn't confuse them once we're all together."

They talk about Maggie. Bitta and Matthew will be looking in on her, but Brian doesn't feel right leaving his mother alone more than a few days. Another "bookmark" conversation to avoid, whether Brian can feasibly relocate to Niagara.

They even tackle the Pinot conversation. Faith admits she has tried a few for work, detecting some cherry and vanilla in some of the dryer versions that impressed her. In the two weeks they've been together, Brian has learned not to push her too hard on his favourite grape. He resists the impulse to add his opinion, giving her a thumbs up.

"I'm looking forward to sampling the Cab Franc," he offers. "SpringSide is getting some mad raves on the 2016 vintage."

By the time they pull into the vineyard, a citrus sun sinks low over grape-lined hills. So far, they've navigated the thorniest issues carefully, putting off the unavoidable decisions ahead of them.

"Where's your apartment?" His eyebrows move up and down, playfully.

Faith laughs and parks in front of the SpringSide shop. "Out back. We just need to stop inside here real quick." She keeps her eyes fixed on her feet as she slides out of the van. She's never been a good liar, and she has a feeling he will see right through her if she looks in his eyes.

Once he's out, she grabs his hand, still avoiding eye contact, tugging him toward the door. "I love a woman in a hurry," he jokes, pushing the door open before she can. "After you, my sweet." He holds the door open and makes a sweeping gesture with his arm.

"Surprise!"

A cacophony of voices push Brian's shoulders back like a wave. "What the…"

Faith squeezes his hand. "Happy Birthday," she says. Across the crowded store, his eyes land on Vivia and Jensen. They sit at a wine tasting counter, smiling widely, their glasses of bubbly aloft.

Maggie bursts from the crowd with two champagne flutes. She hugs Faith. Then her son, wishing him a happy birthday. "Where's the real alcohol?" she whispers.

"I thought I left you back in Ottawa. How'd you…" Brian flounders on the logic.

Bitta sidles up to Faith and kisses her, Matthew trailing behind. "Look at you," Bitta says. She waves her arms all around her. "A real job. You did it." Her voice is breathy.

Faith eyes her carefully. Is her stoic grandmother going to cry?

Bitta swipes at her cheeks before Faith can say anything and turns to Brian. "Happy Birthday, Mister Right." She tries to shake his hand.

He hugs her instead. "Thank you, Bitta. You guys drove all this way? I'm touched."

"Don't get all sentimental on me," Bitta says, straightening. She points over at Matthew, now leaning against a gift display. "This one has a heavy foot. Got us here tout suite."

Spying Allie, Faith makes a beeline toward her. "Man I miss living next door to you!" she says, hugging Allie hard. She nearly knocks over Chad who stands at the tasting bar next to Allie. "Chad! You came!"

Chad's eyes dart from her to Brian, now chatting with Matthew across the room. "Yeah, well, someone has to study up on the wines now that I'm stuck with the displays again."

"You'll do great," Faith says, giving Chad an awkward hug. "Sorry about that date we almost had."

He holds out his glass. "Cheers, curly."

His cheeks are the colour of Rosé. He glances at Allie, who looks down at her feet, sliding onto the barstool behind her as she does so.

"Are you two…?" Faith isn't sure how to finish the question.

Just then, Morty interrupts. "Hey there, hot shot. Hope you like the decorations."

Faith takes in the rainbow of balloons bumping against the ceiling, the Happy Birthday banner draped across a wall mirror, and the spread of glitter twinkling from every shelf and table. "Thanks, Morty. I owe you one."

"Got that right," he teases. "Hey, I want to meet the man of the hour."

"I'll introduce you. C'mon." As she leads him across the room, she notices Stella near a snack table. The rosy-cheeked man next to her must be Ralph. SpringSide's winemaker, owner and staff beam from behind the bar, where they pour sparkling and close out the register. On a barstool, near Vivia and Jensen, sits a man she doesn't recognize. He sips bubbly with his back to the crowd, talking to no one. "Who's that?" she asks Morty, pointing.

"Heck if I know," he says. "He just showed up. I was busy bedazzling the place."

135

Brian envelops her in a hug as soon as she gets to him.

"Get a room!" Jensen yells from the bar.

Brian laughs, then notices the man sitting next to Vivia get up and head his way. He recognizes the hipster glasses.

The man carries a legal-sized envelope, which he hands to Brian, saying "Happy Birthday."

"Hello, Mr. Weiss," Brian says, suddenly serious. "Is this what I think it is?"

"Maximum fine," he says. "And you can still call me Don."

A corner of Brian's mouth curves up. "Well, whatever the fine. It's worth it."

Don pulls out a small box from his inside jacket pocket. It is wrapped in sky blue paper and tied with a yellow bow. Holding it out to Faith, he says, "Nice to meet you, young lady. I hear good things."

"Don works for SoulMate," Brian explains. "Here to collect on my unauthorized contact with you." His face pinches into a grimace. "Post refund."

"Aha," Faith says, glaring at Brian. "Nice to meet you, Don. What's this?"

"Just a token of appreciation for enjoying our service," he says. There's a hint of a smile in his eyes. "All our matches get one."

Don starts to turn away. Brian grabs his shoulder. "How many applicants don't get one?"

Don shakes his head slowly. "I'm not at liberty to say." Then he smiles warmly at Faith. "Still hate Pinot?" he says.

Faith shrugs her shoulders. "Working on it." She leans closer to Don and adds, "He's actually not a chipmunk killer."

Don nods. Before he walks back to the tasting bar, he says to Brian, "Call me if you want to write that exposé from another angle."

"Interesting fellow," Faith says to Brian. She hands him the gift. "It's your birthday."

He laughs, peeling off the bow and paper. Inside a satin-lined box are two golden locks joined together. Faith touches the one with her name etched on it. Brian takes them out. Turns them over in his hands. Etched on the other side, are the words *Soul Mates*.

Faith lifts up the satin liner and shakes the box. "There's no key."

Brian smiles. "Locked together forever."

THE END

ACKNOWLEDGMENTS

Thanks to the organizers of the International 3 Day Novel contest, I discovered that time spent watching "rom com" movies is good for something. Without the creative freedom to write whatever I wanted over Labour Day weekend, I might not have written *Pairs With Pinot*.

Writing it was fun. I weeped with joy when the ending came together less than an hour before the midnight deadline; just like the happy tears I cry at the end of every rom com movie. I am utterly astonished that something so deliciously fun to write earned an international award shortlist spot ten months later. Thank you, 3 Day Novel contest judges, for finding merit in this story.

Thank you Rob Bignell, of Reality Editing, for taking a fine tooth comb to my final draft.

Thank you to all the kind souls who gave valuable feedback during the editing process. Because of you, Faith and Brian are off to a more fulfilling start. Janice Young, Beverly Brinkman, Christine Wheary, Cami Nihipali, and Julianna Thibodeaux, you complete me!

Thank you Bekah Berge for educating me on Old World versus New World Pinot Noir. I learned so much from your knowledge as a sommelier. And Faith's perspective grew as a result.

A cover can make or break a book. Thank you Hanna Piepel, gifted artist, for creating an eye-catching cover that perfectly captures the story of Brian and Faith. Your attention to detail, knowledge of industry trends, and skillful adaptation of your designs to the rom com genre resulted in a truly unique, crowd-pleasing cover.

Thank you, Ines Monnet, formatting genius, for creating a framework of font-to-page aesthetic that's pure magic.

For lending a trained designer eye toward selecting and tweaking my cover options, I'm grateful to Mark and Yasmine Charlton and Sabrina Quraeshi. I could not have chosen between Hanna Piepel's equally beautiful designs without your help.

For all the friends, family and neighbours who rarely complain when I drag you to see every romantic comedy that hits the theatre, thank you. You know who you are!

Last but not least, thank you Alan, my actual soulmate, for all you do behind the scenes so I can write. You had me at hello when we met over a game of Euchre. You are the reason I believe in happily ever after.

THANK YOU FOR READING!

If you enjoyed my story, please leave a review and tell your friends! The best way to help authors is to leave a review on amazon.com. You can also copy and paste your review onto goodreads.com .

And don't forget to share your review with friends!
Use the hashtag #PairsWithPinot on Instagram or Twitter.

CONNECT!

Tell me what you think.

Ask me a question.

Find out when to expect a second instalment in the Love and Wine Series.

I love hearing from my readers!

Website: maryanntippett.ca
Instagram: @maryanntippett
Twitter: @maryanntip
BookBub: Mary Ann Tippett

Made in the USA
Lexington, KY
21 December 2019